The pavilion was supposed to be a replica of an "entertainment" room of an ancient Turkish palace, but to Sam Durell it looked more like a five-minute brothel. It was big, noisy, gaudy, and alive with flashing lights.

The place was jammed—mostly with big-bosomed, nearly naked, jiggling Eurasian dancers. It would have been one of Durell's most enjoyable moments—if he hadn't been busy trying to outrun a gang of gigantic bronzed bodyguards dressed in costumes right out of the most lascivious Arabian Nights stories ... the ones they don't print in the collections for Americans.

As Durell raced through the girls' dressing room and toward a small door at the end, an almost naked blonde suddenly appeared and beckoned to him. "In here," she whispered. "Quickly."

He dived past her and she slammed the door shut.

She grabbed him and kissed him, and he caught only a glimpse of shining glass and steel as she drove a hypodermic into the back of his neck ...

Assignment..... The Cairo Dancers

Edward S. Aarons

CORONET BOOKS
Hodder Fawcett Ltd., London

Printed and bound in Great Britain for
Coronet Books,
Hodder Fawcett Ltd,
St. Paul's House, Warwick Lane,
London, E.C.4
by Hazell Watson & Viney Ltd,
Aylesbury, Bucks

ISBN 0 340 15187 0

ASSIGNMENT.....
THE CAIRO DANCERS

Chapter One

IN ROME one day in early spring, Dr. Paolo Nardinocchi vanished. It was not intentional. He did not know it was all prepared for him. But on that day—or rather night, for that was when he indulged his weakness—he disappeared utterly.

It was a rainy evening, and he liked to walk along the Via Veneto and look at the American tourists crowding the Excelsior, the movie stars in their spectacular dark glasses, and the glamorous women and parasitical men of Roman café society. They were as far removed from Dr. Paolo Nardinocchi's life as if they lived on Mars—which, indeed, was closer to the doctor's understanding than these elegant, chattering people at their café tables.

He was in a hurry. He had a wife and two teen-age daughters and a fine apartment rent-free, thanks to the Optical Institute—which received mysterious subsidies from the American Government for Dr. Nardinocchi's work—but he was not heading for home and family that rainy, romantic spring night.

He was going to see Gina.

Gina was a late-blooming orchid in the good doctor's life, a last brightening of a dying flame within his male ego. Until he met Gina, he thought of himself as a respectable, bearded, middle-aged scientist slightly bored with the emotional storms exhibited by his children, who were tasting the first lusts and languors of life. Gina changed all that. He had to admit he was behaving worse than the most irresponsible youth.

But Dr. Paolo Nardinocchi did not care.

At fifty-seven, he was in love with all the fervor and violence of a colt, ignoring home, wife, children and work. And it was all for Gina.

She was dark and voluptuous and dedicated to the sole proposition that life was equated with pleasure. He did not know where she came from, and he did not care, as long as she did not depart. He was already heavily in debt because of her. He was a slave to her sleek, smooth, sinuous body. When he visioned her ripe breasts and clasping thighs, he would be beside himself, unable to work, eat, think, or do anything but run to her—as he did on this rainy, romantic night in Rome.

"Paolo," she sighed. "*Carissimo,* you are late."

He gasped in relief. "Gina, you waited."

"Of course, Paolo. I promised you I would wait one more day, did I not?" She pouted, and her ripe mouth was the essence of an orgy, a red riot of paradise. She kissed his left ear and lifted herself from the divan. "But I am not one to risk poverty, dear Paolo. It would kill me, literally."

"It will not happen," he breathed.

"Dear Paolo, of course not. You brought the items?"

"Yes. Yes, I did. It was very dangerous. But I—I need some wine, something to drink—"

"Where are they?" Gina asked.

"The papers? In the attaché case—over there."

"Ah, good," she said. "This will be worth a lot of money, and I shall be rich."

"But you will stay here in Rome?"

"Of course, Paolo, pet." She looked at him with long, green eyes, and he remembered how she had danced for him the other night, all alone, for him alone, enchanting and wildly lustful, until he thought his heart would burst with desire for her. Anything she wanted, anything, was hers. He could not and would not lose her. He watched her slide toward him, her green eyes great and generous with promise as she said, "Paolo, could anyone understand such mysteries, other than you? Your work is so complicated, such a terribly important and brilliant project—"

"I could explain the formulae, of course—"

"Could anyone else?"

"I am not certain. But let us not talk of my work—"

"If no one could understand it, of what value are the papers?"

"I don't know. You said you could get money for them, and although I know I am selling my soul for you, Gina, I stole them, and they are yours."

She pouted. "But perhaps they are worthless, without you to explain them."

"That may be so."

8

"Then you will have to go along with them, will you not dear Paolo?"

"I do not understand—"

"You will," she promised "*Ciao*, darling."

And her eyes were pools of drowning sadness as she plunged the little needle into the nape of his fat neck.

Dr. Paolo Nardinocchi fell instantly unconscious.

And he was never seen again.

That summer, Professor Anton Novotnik was taken in quite another way.

He wanted to defect to the West.

He remembered old Czechoslovakia, in the days before the Hitler regime, and the subsequent Soviet tidal wave that had submerged his busy, industrial little country and transformed it into a drab and miserable wasteland. He loved Prague, so of course *They* did not permit him to work there; instead, he was stationed in Bratislava, on the gray and chilly Danube, in the optical laboratories sponsored by Project Sunbeam.

Professor Novotnik thought the code name was a grisly jest.

But he was devoted to his work and grateful that he was permitted to continue with it. It was important enough to shake the world. Like Archimedes, if he were successful, he could well move the world, not with a lever, but with a ray of sunlight. Still, he hated his Soviet masters and the Czech puppets who profited from his labors and sucked the juices of his genius.

Freedom was only the width of a river away, across the Danube in Austria.

That summer he was offered escape, and he took it.

A man who soon identified himself, most carefully, as an American—though he seemed a Levantine to Novotnik, who knew, however, that America was a melting pot and that there were all sorts of people from all over the world who were U. S. citizens, indeed, did he not hope to become one himself—this man offered him escape from Bratislava to freedom across the river.

"We can do it tonight, Professor. It is one of those warm nights when the Danube is covered with mist."

"Yes, and on such nights the patrols are doubled and re-doubled," said Anton grimly.

"That will be taken care of."

9

"How?"

The "American" laughed. "Do I ask you how you run your laboratory, Professor? Would I understand it, even if you tried to explain it to me?"

"No, I suppose not," said Anton.

"Then don't ask me the details of my business."

"But," said Anton practically, "I am placing my life in your hands."

"You will lose nothing," said the stranger, laughing, "but your chains."

Professor Novotnik thought it was an unhappy paraphrase of the Communist slogan for the world's workers. But he went along with it. He was eager for freedom. He saw no real menace in this new-found friend, this young man who risked his own life behind the Iron Curtain just to save him, out of respect for his intellect and scientific achievements. The professor was something of an egotist, and his opinion of himself, however warranted, was often swollen beyond the reaches of common sense; hence his unscientific approach to this nameless man who promised him escape from the dreary world of Communist enterprise.

It was an appropriately foggy night when the attempt to cross the Danube was made. The American's face was always vague, and seemed cruel and hard, with the cruelty of young people, the professor thought, and the hardness of someone confident of his own strength.

"You don't want to see your wife, do you, Professor?" asked his guide, as they waited on the foggy riverfront.

"No."

"She might give you away, eh?"

"She would. She is a devoted Party member, a fanatic. They call her the 'Hanging Judge,' you know," said Professor Novotnik, and he shuddered.

The American chuckled. "Question is, Anton, are you running from the Reds because of all we promised you, or are you just running away from your wife?"

"Something of both, I suppose," Anton said wearily. "Where is the boat? It is late."

"Don't get nervous. Did you bring your extracts?"

Anton patted his worn briefcase. "It is all here, all the data I've been working on."

"Good. You won't regret it."

The last thing Professor Anton Novotnik saw was the Danube waterfront, with the gloomy piles of Bratislava's river

10

industries looming weirdly in the night mist. Beyond the oily, dirty waters of the Danube was Austria, far, far from sight.

He never saw it.

The needle gave only an instant of pain, and then he fell down at the "American's" feet and knew nothing more.

And he, too, vanished.

The third disappearance was Dr. Hubertus Steigmann, whose last address was Huntsville, Alabama, U.S.A.

By now it was autumn.

In Hubertus Steigmann's case, the lure was not the bait of warm and willing flesh, as with Dr. Nardinocchi in Rome, or the promise of freedom in some bright western horizon, as with Novotnik in Bratislava. In Steigmann's case, both the whip and the carrot were used.

The whip was an ancient murder charge that he thought was completely unknown to anyone in the world. It was an especially brutal and unnatural crime. He had killed his own brother, and never regretted it.

But someone knew.

The carrot was his daughter, Lisl. He didn't know she was still alive, until she wrote very guardedly to him. The letter reached him secretly, and it left Hubertus in an abnormal state of emotion and remorse and a vast expansion of paternal love for a twenty-two-year-old daughter he had never once seen. Everything he had tried to forget came back to him like a torrent of water sweeping through the fissures of a burst dam.

Dr. Steigmann had been given probationary clearance by the CIA personnel division long ago, as a refugee, and the same rating had been granted by the Federal Bureau of Investigation, in charge of domestic security, when they probed his past in East Germany, twenty years ago. There were no papers anywhere to prove or disprove anything, and the skimpy dossiers had grown yellow in the files in Washington by the time this autumn rolled around. Dr. Steigmann was now a naturalized American citizen, familiar to the readers of scientific journals and a popular lecturer at engineering conventions. If there was no hint or proof of evil or subversive politics in his distant past, there was also no proof of his innocence. But he was on the verge of a vital breakthrough, and his contribution to America's defense would

11

vindicate the tentative clearance he had been granted in war-torn Berlin almost a quarter-century ago.

Steigmann seemed to be a gentle man. He tried not to appear sentimental, and the staff who worked under him at the laser laboratories in Huntsville hardly thought of him as a romantic. But *They* discovered this and located Lisl, his daughter, and took it from there.

After that, it was quite simple.

Dr. Steigmann flew to attend a joint Anglo-American conference on the imminent breakthrough promised by his work, and from London, he found an excuse to visit Edinburgh University for a day's research. Security was both lax and complacent. No one saw him take the BEA jet to Munich that autumn afternoon, and no one even knew he had gone back to Germany, after all those years, until lurid headlines broke in the newspapers of Western Europe about his capture and arrest by the German Federal authorities as a long-wanted war criminal and high Nazi official guilty of the most monstrous crimes during the darkest days of the Hitler regime.

As if that were not enough, on the second day of Dr. Steigmann's imprisonment—he escaped.

And Dr. Steigmann, like his fellow workers, Dr. Nardinocchi and Professor Novotnik, completely vanished, too.

That was when it came to Sam Durell.

Chapter Two

DURELL flew to Huntsville for two days, then took a jet back to Washington and No. 20 Annapolis Street, headquarters for K Section of the Central Intelligence Agency. He was a field agent for K Section, with a sub-chief rating in this troubleshooting department whose budgetary details were buried in General Accounting, and whose boss, General Dickinson McFee, reported directly to the National Security Agency, Joint Chiefs, and the White House.

The day was one of those hot, humid September days in Washington when air-conditioners overheated and blew fuses and tempers were held under minimum control. General McFee, that small, haunted gray man, was the only person Durell met who looked cool.

"Sit down, Cajun," McFee said. "There won't be much time ahead for you in which to rest."

"It's always hurry-up-and-wait," said Durell.

"This time, however, we have to hurry, and we can't wait. All the signals are red. Everywhere."

"I couldn't dig up a thing on the missing Dr. Hubertus Steigmann—not down in Huntsville, anyway."

"Steigmann is only one thread in a very tangled skein, Cajun. But he's a thread we may be able to pull on and get to the center of the knot. We've perceived a pattern now, and it's damned serious. The missing Herr Doctor, if I may mix metaphors, may be the detonating cap to a bundle of dynamite."

Durell was silent. McFee rarely spoke this way, and he felt a cold squirm in the pit of his stomach while he waited. McFee pushed dossiers with red tags signaling URGENT across the desk toward Durell, who did not touch them yet.

"You can read these, Sam. In brief, they cover over fourteen major disappearances of top men from everywhere in the world. I'm not just talking about Americans, British or Italians. We've lost Steigmann, and he's the last we know of, but before that there was Wilde-Evans from Wales, and Señor Alvarez from Brazil, Jacques Rondville in Paris, a young Chinese genius named Sung Laio from Taipeh, Nardinocchi out of Rome—well, I could go on and on. We thought at first these were defectors responding to a new pattern, a fresh sort of bait. But we can't find a trace of them in the East. Neither in Moscow, nor in Peking. Not a word out of them. And we've gotten three feelers from your counterparts in the KGB, Sam."

"Then Moscow is missing people, too?"

"Some pretty good ones. The last was Novotnik, the Czech expert on molecular light control. He left word he was defecting out of good conscience to the West and going over to Austria for refuge. But he never got there."

"Any others?"

"Four more from Russia. Two from Red China. The dossiers are there. Somebody is picking brains, Sam—picking and collecting them, right?"

Durell waited again.

"We want Steigmann back, of course. He's important. I don't know what the charges were against him in Germany.

13

If he's really a fugitive war criminal, we'll work that out later. But we want him back with all the information he took from the Huntsville laser laboratories. I know how you feel about war criminals, Sam. They've got something on Steigmann, over in Munich, that we don't have. Our records on him are clean."

"Could he have been framed over there?"

"I think so. Maybe there's some fire under the smoke, though. We're not infallible. We screen people like Steigmann as well as we can—but they come to us, stateless, without passports, penniless. So who can tell? I'll leave it all to your discretion."

"What is that, sir?"

"If you can't bring him back alive, you may have to kill him."

"I see."

"But most of all, Sam, whatever underground railway is operating to spirit brains out of the laboratories of the world, you've got to find that railroad. Find it, and follow Steigmann if he was maneuvered aboard, buy a ticket on it, and ride it to its final destination."

Durell said: "They wouldn't let me in the station, so to speak. I'm not a scientist."

"I don't care how you get aboard this underground railway, Sam. That's up to you. But you must find the other terminal. Be a decoy. Play it dumb. Blunder about a bit." McFee looked haunted. "Of course, Cajun, you could get killed that way."

"I'll try not to let that happen, General."

Chapter Three

HE READ copies of the dossiers on his flight to London, concentrating on Dr. Steigmann's records, but the files showed little more than what McFee had told him. He burned the records in the plane's lavatory and flushed the ashes into space over the Atlantic. In London, he spoke to shocked research technicians who expressed horror over Steigmann's arrest, escape, and disappearance in Munich. None of it helped. He went to Edinburgh. The trail was cold there.

Steigmann had contacted no one before boarding a BEA jet to Munich. So he moved on to Germany.

Within an hour after he arrived in Munich, Durell knew he was being followed. This pleased him, and he was careful to do nothing to confuse his shadow. Until this moment, he felt he was running down a blind alley in the wrong maze, but now he knew the correct route was near the girl, whom he picked out as his shadow.

He did not think she was dangerous, at first. Her technique was clumsy, so he spotted her easily. He doubled back and learned she was staying at a mediocre place called the Hotel Prinz and that her name was Carole Bainbury and she used a British passport. On the other hand, it was so easy that he began to think she was being clumsy by intent. If she were only pretending to be an amateur and *wanted* to be spotted, then he might be less pleased with himself. He decided to be more careful.

At the same time, he felt better, because it was always easier on the conscience to deal with a professional instead of an outsider. You never knew when someone might need killing, and he did not relish amateurs mixing into the business.

When he had been in Munich for twenty-four hours, he called the K Section field man, using the prescribed formula, and arranged a meet. He went to the reconstructed Peterskirche when a white disc was posted on the northern side of the tower, which meant that visibility was clear all the way to the Alps; if the signal for tourists had been a red ball, indicating visibility limited only to the city, he'd have had to wait one more day. Up in the tower, basking in the September sunshine with the autumnal tourists churning about in excited, beery groups, he spotted Henry Gordon, a bald and tweedy man smoking a meerschaum pipe. They stared at the floating Alpine peaks on the horizon while they talked.

"Where did you first spot her?" Gordon asked.

"At the Platzl Inn, opposite the Hofbrauhaus," Durell told him. "Drinking beer, naturally. What else do you drink in Munich?"

Gordon puffed quietly on his pipe. "This Carole Bainbury who's following you has an M.A. from London University. She's British, right enough, aged twenty-six, and an archaeology aide. She was with the Dudley-Smythe expedition dig-

15

ging up Nabatean cultural remnants in the Negev Desert. Is any of that pertinent, Sam?"

"I don't know yet," Durell said.

"We have nothing critical on her. Ostensibly, she's on an autumn holiday, doing the Continent."

"A very English type," said Durell.

"Very. Tweed skirt and horn-rimmed secretarial glasses. Probably eyestrain from peering at all those dusty, ancient shards, what? She's a cataloguist, whatever that may be, and she's been in Germany for two weeks. This was before our subject flew here, eh? Which might or might not mean anything."

"I think it does. What about the British M.I.6? Could she be working for them?" Durell asked.

"Can't say. I checked it out, of course. They won't give anything away. They never heard of her. Of course, they might change their tune tomorrow. That's the way the game is played, right? As for Carole, I got a physical rundown: plain brown hair, brown eyes, good legs, a hint of a helluva figure under that heavy Scottish skirt." Gordon grinned. The K Section resident agent looked like a pleasant business-man; his record included ten years as a professional espionage field chief. He had killed a top-priority opposite number in a Soviet *apparat* working last year in Geneva, and he should have been pulled back to the States to cool off. But they were all shorthanded, Durell reflected, and some of the people in his own group hadn't gotten contract renewals, so Gordon was kept on. It was risky, but necessary. Gordon was tough and competent, and his cover job in Munich was to run an auto export house for Mercedes-Benz. He added: "That's all I can get on Miss Bainbury just now, Cajun." He looked at the distant Alps from the Peterskirche tower and turned lazily, elbow on the parapet, to consider the slowly moving throngs of tourists up here for the view. "Shall we take her in today and ask her why she's so interested in you, Cajun?"

"Of course not. I want to know who she operates for."

"No one, as far as we can tell."

"Dig a little deeper, Henry."

Gordon said: "You're edgy, old man. Are you in such a big hurry?"

"The biggest."

Gordon raised bushy black brows that contrasted with his bald scalp. "I gather we close this one quickly, or we're all

16

verdammt, eh? I'll scoop deeper into the mud pie, then."

"Don't waste time sleeping," Durell suggested.

At the Platzl Inn the night before, only an hour after his arrival, amid the usual Bavarian singing and dancing, he had definitely confirmed his suspicion that the tall, meek-looking English girl—whose glowing tan betrayed many months in the deserts of the Middle East—was following him. He had walked out into the balmy September night and gone down the Orlando Strasse and then through an archway to the Alter Hof, that ancient homestead of the Dukes of Bavaria. She followed along at a discreet distance behind him. But nicely bred, scholarly English types do not usually stroll about strange foreign cities without an escort. Durell went into the brightly lighted confusion of Marienplatz in the center of Munich, and down Kaufinger Strasse to let her stare at the glittering and prosperous shop windows that reflected the booming economy of the West German Federal Republic. She did the bit perfectly, and seemed to lose him for a time in the traffic flow of fat-cat Mercedes sedans that almost outnumbered the beetle VW's. Then she popped up again outside the Frauenkirche. He shook her there, doubled back through an alley, and became the hunter instead of the hunted.

He watched her from the shadows of a medieval doorway as she took off her black-rimmed glasses and bit the end of one bar in perplexity. She had strong, white teeth. Then she shrugged and adjusted her big shoulder bag—he would have liked to go through that kit and see what sort of weapons she carried—and she took off briskly, her sensible heels rapping smartly on the cobblestones, and retired to the modest Hotel Prinz near the Bahnhofplatz and the railroad station.

It was too easy to follow her, and this was when he grew suspicious that he might be doing precisely what she wished him to do.

But he didn't mind.

Perhaps she could get him a ticket on the invisible railroad he was seeking.

Chapter Four

HE HAD checked in at the Bayerischer Hof, one of Munich's luxury hotels, and after leaving Gordon he returned there and ordered all the local newspapers sent to his room, along with the London *Times* and the Paris edition of the *Herald Tribune*. The day remained sunny and sparkling. The flurry of sensation over Dr. Hubertus Steigmann's arrest, escape and vanishment was dying down in the press. It always did, Durell reflected. One could not and must not embarrass the Federal Republic, even though the German tribunal in Karlsruhe that handled war-crime trials had become as matter-of-fact and casual as a municipal traffic court.

He waited until eleven o'clock for Inspector Bellau, of the West German Federal Intelligence Service, to telephone him. But the telephone remained silent.

He did not like this.

Durell was a tall man, with a heavy musculature and thick black hair touched by gray at the temples. He had a lean and careful face, with blue eyes that turned black when he was angry or impatient. He had been in espionage for a long time—sometimes he thought it had been too long—and he tried not to tag himself with personal idiosyncrasies in dress or habit. He wore inconspicuous dark suits, white button-down shirts, dark knitted neckties. Aside from his height, and the way he carried himself—which a trained observer could identify as the walk of a dangerous man—he could lose himself in most crowds. He preferred bourbon and the chicory-flavored coffee native to the bayous of his home in Louisiana. But aside from these personal tastes, he was adaptable to all the ordinary habits of any country he happened to visit.

He had been a sub-chief for K Section long enough to know that his survival factor had worn precariously thin. As a troubleshooter, he operated in all the strange corners of the world, usually with a team, but preferably alone. He worked, ate, slept and made love in the perpetual shadows of danger.

The telephone did not ring.

He had undergone a bitter training to get rid of his Cajun drawl and overlay it with a faint New England nasality picked up with his law degree at Yale. He spoke a number of languages and dialects with varying degrees of familiarity. The training at the Farm, in Maryland, included varied methods of murder, as well as a psychological indoctrination that made you suspicious and quite alone in a world henceforth regarded as hostile. He could kill with a rolled newspaper, a pencil, the edge of his palm, a roll of coins, a sewing needle held between thumb and forefinger. It was a matter of knowing the precise, vital neural centers of the human anatomy. His hands were strong, as clever as a gambler's—and he had learned all the tricks of gambling from his Grandpa Jonathan, as a boy, back in the hot shadows of Bayou Peche Rouge. Old Jonathan had been one of the last of the Mississippi riverboat gamblers. He had made Durell what he was—a man who could hunt other men and who, in turn, was not afraid to be hunted.

It set him apart. He could have taken a desk job in Analysis and Synthesis at No. 20 Annapolis Street, working up extrapolations for Joint Chiefs and the White House, but he couldn't go back across the gulf that separated him from everyday life. Each year, the notations on his contract renewal offered a recall from field work, but he could not return. He had become different from other men.

In Moscow, in the square named after Felix Dzerzhinsky, a Russian Bolshevist born in Poland in 1877 and the founder of the dreaded Cheka and OGPU, Durell's record was on file in the offices of the KGB. This was at No. 2 Dzerzhinsky Square, opposite the ill-famed Lubyanka Prison. His dossier was marked with a red tab, and both the MVD and the "Center" of the *Kommissariat Gosudarstvennoi Bezopastnotsi*—the KGB, Commissariat of State Security—had a remarkably complete account of his work, according to a CIA cell who had reported on it seven months ago. (The cell was executed not long after his microfilm report was passed through the Berlin Wall.) Nothing in that red-tagged file promised Durell a long or peaceful life.

The telephone rang at 11:27.

"Herr Durell?"

"I am here," Durell replied in German.

"I must beg your pardon for the delay. Please understand, we have been very busy, and we are shorthanded."

19

"Who isn't? But go ahead, Inspector Bellau. I assume this line isn't bugged?"

"Bugged? Oh, yes. Rather, I mean, it is not."

"But you are taping this conversation?"

"It is routine, sir, so there will be no misunderstanding in the future about our cooperation." Bellau paused. "We have found the missing prison guard who helped Steigmann escape. But, alas, the man is dead."

Durell was not surprised. "Was he eliminated?"

"It seems to be suicide."

"Remorse?"

"It is possible."

"But not probable. I want to see the body."

"Naturally. I will be at your hotel in a few minutes. You will be ready?"

"I'm ready now."

Inspector Franz Bellau picked him up in the usual black Mercedes sedan in front of the hotel on the Promenadeplatz. Bellau was not as cheerful as the sparkling September sunshine. He could be classified as a dwarf, but seated on the plush gray seat of the car, giving the uniformed chauffeur an address beyond the suburbs of Munich, he seemed of normal height, except for an over-large head and thin neck. He had protruding, yellowish eyes, and he wore gray suede gloves and a flowing blue-polka-dot ascot tie, and carried a sword-cane that qualified as an antique from the days of Frederick III.

In Munich's suburb of Pullach, there was a building compound surrounded by high concrete walls which enclosed the headquarters of the West German Federal Intelligence Service. The FIS cooperated closely with the CIA, which here was known simply as the "Special Detachment." In this fortress of intrigue commanded by a man called the "Gray Colonel"—who had somehow survived de-Nazification—Inspector Bellau was secure behind his Atlantic Wall of secret files. His physique prohibited any field work, and Bellau's temperament made him unsuited for such, in any case. His mind and memory were like electronic computers; his cold and analytical brain sought survival first, last, and always. It was said in the business that Bellau's memory could indict half of Bonn, if he were moved to reveal all that was hidden in his secret dossiers.

The heavy car sped swiftly and luxuriously through the

busy streets of Munich. Bellau closed the sliding glass between the rear seat and the driver, using the delicate tip of his gleaming stick, and said: "We have complete privacy, Herr Durell. You may speak freely to me."

"How many bugs are rigged in the car?" Durell asked. He reached for the flowers in a small glass vase beside the door and plucked out a tiny microphone no larger than his thumbnail. "Is the tape recorder in the back trunk?"

Inspector Bellau smiled and took the blue blossom from Durell and tucked it in his lapel. His lower lip was stained by tobacco, but he was not smoking now. "We must keep an official record of our conversations, my dear Durell."

"But I'm not here, officially."

"True. But the Special Detachment makes demands of my office that must be recognized."

"What I'm here to do is to find Dr. Hubertus Steigmann and take him back to the States," Durell said.

"I wish I could produce him for you. The task is not easy. Or as simple as you pretend." Bellau's yellow eyes were amused. "How, if I may be impertinent, did Hubertus Steigmann ever get away from you, over in America, in the first place? You will forgive me if I sound cynical."

"Let us not cast stones, Herr Inspector, or call the kettle black. We use whatever tools come to hand. Dr. Steigmann worked at Huntsville for eighteen years as an expert on optics. We knew that he's not yet in his sixties, and that his wife was killed by a Soviet tank that knocked his house to rubble in Berlin. But we had no record of his living daughter over here. He was a solitary man, devoted to his work, and seemed satisfactory on all counts."

"We know," Bellau said, "that he made remarkable advances in laser development."

Durell looked at the fastidious dwarf. "True."

"Your press, Herr Durell, is a source of vital information for every espionage department in the world. From that viewpoint, your open society has many faults. One of your more sensational New York tabloids called Dr. Steigmann the 'Father of the Death Ray.'"

"We don't control our press as you do, Inspector. You put your finger on it before. We have a free society."

"Too free, perhaps. But I should not criticize. America has been more than generous to those she has conquered. Witness our prosperity and the manner in which we have been—ah—forgiven our alleged crimes."

21

Durell said nothing.

Bellau added mildly: "It is true that Steigmann was a wanted war criminal who vanished completely from our records. We assumed the Soviets had him and closed our files. The puzzle is, why did he risk returning to Germany from the safety of your laboratories in Huntsville, Alabama? One would not expect sentiment in such a man."

"I hold no brief for Steigmann," said Durell. "If he's guilty of atrocities in the past, he should be punished as the courts prescribe."

"We abase ourselves in our guilt. We heap ashes of remorse on our heads," Bellau murmured.

Durell's eyes were dark and cold. "Steigmann's record is clean as far as we can determine. He was cleared for a conference at London University involving laser and maser beam developments. He was kept under surveillance during a side trip to Edinburgh last week, but he got away from our people and took a plane for Munich. We had no information about his daughter or his sentiment for her." He paused. "It seems to me that if Steigmann were guilty of wartime atrocities, he would have changed his name twenty years ago in order to hide his identity. Since he didn't, he's either naïve or foolish, and I don't think he's either. Until he's proved guilty, therefore, we must consider him as innocent."

"But his own daughter denounced him, my dear fellow! A lovely young woman, full of her German guilt. We know Hubertus visited her. Is it usual for a daughter to charge her father with the vicious crimes of working electronic experiments on prison-camp inmates in Poland?" Bellau sighed and sniffed at his boutonniere and gave a brief order to the driver through a speaking tube. The sleek car turned into a wide thoroughfare and headed west in the sparkling noon. Bellau added: "As for Fräulein Lisl Steigmann's denunciation of her father, one must remember her youth, her indoctrination in our nation's guilt, and her desire to atone for the crimes we committed."

"Did your office have all this data about Steigmann's record in Poland? Was all this in your files?"

"Of course, Herr Durell. But we thought he was dead."

Durell sighed, too. "All right. Steigmann came to Munich, presumably on a sentimental journey to see a daughter he had abandoned in her infancy. She turned against him, shocked by his rising from the grave, so to speak, and called your headquarters at Pullach and denounced him. The war-crimes tribunal at Karlsruhe was informed, and he was arrested."

Bellau spread his elegantly gloved hands. "What else could we do? Fräulein Lisl also called the newspapers."

"Yes. And the first night Steigmann was held in custody, the guard, a man named Hans Dorpler, a former SS sergeant, allowed him to escape. And Dorpler vanished after him."

"So it seems."

"And Dr. Steigmann, with a head full of laser data, and especially the details of a new model—"

"The 'death ray,'" Bellau said. He smiled coldly. "It is amusing how we grow immune to the enormous threats that hang over humanity, Herr Durell."

"It is not amusing to us. In any case, we want Steigmann back. But you have found no trace of him at all?"

"We found something this morning," Bellau told him. "We found Hans Dorpler, the guard you mentioned, the man who betrayed us by letting Steigmann escape and go free."

"And it's Dorpler who is dead?"

"Precisely."

Chapter Five

IT SEEMED to Durell that Bellau held back more than he gave, but this was one of the rules of the business. He settled back and wondered how Lisl Steigmann had known about her father's past, if Steigmann's records were dusty and buried in Bellau's files. She'd been an infant when Steigmann had fled to America. Someone must have informed her of her father's alleged history. Bellau? Durell held judgment in abeyance, but he wondered why the Germans, so thorough and efficient, hadn't hunted for Steigmann in the U. S. laboratories in Huntsville, Alabama. Surely, Bellau hadn't slipped up there in the hunt for war criminals. He wondered again why Steigmann, if he were guilty of the crimes Bellau said he was guilty of, hadn't changed his name twenty years ago to elude the hunt. Durell saw the whole pattern of Steigmann's risky trip to Germany, his denunciation, imprisonment, and carefully planned escape simply as a complex operation to snare the man onto the underground railway. Others had taken the same route before him. But—to where? He had no idea. And he kept his doubts about Bellau to himself.

The heavy car crossed the Isar, from Zweibrücken Strasse, with the sprawl of the Deutsches Science Museum off to their right. Durell looked backward. A red VW had followed them from the center of the city, and he did not think it was an accident. The Mercedes hissed into the countryside, lifted smoothly over a stone bridge, and slid down a lane of beech trees turning copper in the autumn sun. Farms flashed by, and then a wooded area, and in the center of the woods they rolled through the medieval gates of an enormous country house with an iron-fenced courtyard and a baroque fountain centered among Belgian cobbles. Tall windows glinted in the bright sunshine as they halted.

"What place is this?" Durell asked.

"It is a hospital for the defective and crippled." Bellau's yellow eyes shone like the leaves that stirred in the warm breeze that swept the areaway of the *Schloss*. A man in a leather apron and a police officer came through the central doorway. "It was set up for victims from the concentration camps, and then continued as a hospital for them and their dependents."

"And the guard who let Steigmann escape—was he found here?" Durell's memory flicked through reports and dossiers. "Isn't Fräulein Lisl Steigmann connected with this place?"

"It was mentioned in the newspapers. At six o'clock this morning, Hans Dorpler, the missing guard, slipped into Fräulein Lisl's apartment. This estate belonged to her maternal grandparents, you see. She has atoned for her father's guilt by turning over the family house to the Federal Government, which pays for its upkeep now. She works with the chief medical administrator. A lovely, charming girl—but a bit too intense, if you understand me."

The policeman opened the car door and saluted respectfully, his eyes careful as the tiny Inspector swung to the cobblestones. Bellau handled his walking stick like a Victorian dandy, adjusted his flowing blue scarf, and walked with a rolling gait on tiny, bandy legs toward the *Schloss* entrance. More policemen appeared and saluted his grotesque figure. A sergeant walked with them down a tiled corridor and past medical offices to a central hallway hung with medieval banners of ancient Bavarian baronies.

24

"The fugitive, Hans Dorpler, slipped into the girl's tower apartment at five this morning, Herr Inspector. He held Fräulein Lisl terrorized as he implored her to help. He said he had aided her father's escape in order to save Germany's honor and keep further disgraceful trials from blackening our good name. He seemed paranoiac, the fräulein said, as if he still clung to National Socialist philosophy; he seemed to live in the past glories of military triumphs. As the fräulein put it, Dorpler was an 'unredeemed Nazi.'" The sergeant spoke with the cynicism of an educated man, his eyes sliding to watch Durell's reaction. "When Dorpler realized that Lisl Steigmann would not sympathize with him, and that she meant to turn him over to the police, he jumped from her tower window—she says."

"Shocking," Bellau murmured.

Durell said: "Didn't Fräulein Lisl learn where her father might be?"

"No, sir. Dorpler told her nothing about this."

"I want to talk to the girl."

"I am sorry, sir; she is not here. She told her story to a medical aide, and when he ran down to the courtyard to look at Dorpler's body, she slipped out of her rooms and drove away in her car. We cannot find her. She has vanished as completely as her father."

A dark blanket covered the body as it sprawled on the cobblestones under a high, round tower of the *Schloss*. The red ivy that climbed the walls matched the ooze of blood that had seeped from under the covering. Inspector Bellau delicately moved the blanket aside with the tip of his walking stick and considered the dead man's face. It had not been damaged by the fall, except for a froth of pinkness in the open mouth. It was just a face, heavy-jowled, with hair like iron-gray wires. Dorpler still wore his prison-guard uniform.

The breeze died and Durell sniffed and dropped to his knees beside the corpse and sniffed again.

"Hashish?"

Bellau said: "It is not common here."

"Common enough in other places."

"It is possible."

"Had he any Arab friends?"

"We will check. You are right. He was under the influence of drugs when he fell. The smell is obvious. As you Americans say, he was flying high." Bellau smiled.

Durell looked up at the high tower.

"A little too high. Have an autopsy made."

"Yes. I am annoyed the girl has disappeared."

Leaves blew across the courtyard and gathered in small waves around the dead man's feet. Durell looked up again at the rounded tower walls and saw an open window up high. One of the policemen said the window was in the girl's apartment. They went up there.

This wing was set aside for staff quarters. The corridors were antiseptic. An ornate stairway led to the tower apartment. Another guard stood at the door to Lisl Steigmann's rooms. They were small and neat, with narrow windows overlooking the courtyard where a fountain sprayed fronds of water over green, fat-buttocked cupids. The smell of hashish smoke still lingered here. It took Durell back to certain Arab cafés he had visited in Algiers. Bellau picked up a cigarette butt and held it delicately between his fingers and nodded and put it away. Hans Dorpler had jumped or fallen or been pushed to his death from here. But Durell accepted nothing he saw. He felt that everything was too smooth; they were too anxious to please him.

Inspector Bellau dropped him at his Munich hotel shortly after noon. He ordered a lunch that would have been far too heavy, had he eaten it all; he refused the rich dessert and chose a tall glass of lager. The studious man at the next table was one of Bellau's people, but he didn't mind. There were no messages at the hotel desk. He chose a public phone and called Gordon at his auto export agency. The CIA resident listened in silence as Durell brought him up to date.

"It may be a cover-up," Durell said. "The girl has the answers. I want to find her before Bellau gets her."

"You think Dorpler told her where to find her father?"

"No. If she turned Steigmann in the first time, she'd do it again. I think she ran off in panic."

He told Gordon what to do, and hung up. For twenty minutes he mixed with the crowd on Munich's busy downtown streets, exerting all his skill to shake off any shadows, while Gordon used the time to fill his end of the task. It was a question of flushing the hare out of the bramble bush.

Eventually he stood behind the service entrance of the Hotel Prinz, where Carole Bainbury had taken up residence. Gordon's job was to enter the front way, threaten her with immediate arrest, then retreat. The object was to make her run.

She showed in three minutes. The street was narrow, with antique shops in tall, medieval houses fronted by baroque façades. The brown-haired girl slipped from the hotel doorway and looked both ways, her face taut. Then, with a tweedy coat swinging open from her fine shoulders, she struck off for the Marienplatz. Durell appreciated her good legs as he followed. She took a taxi to the English Garden, sat on a bench for ten minutes, then jumped up and walked again in search of another taxi. Her destination was a block of middle-class apartments near the river. Durell was only ten seconds behind her when she went inside.

The inner door was closing when he caught it and kept the latch from shutting him out. Miss Bainbury's sensible shoes betrayed her on the stairs above. He gave her time to round the second landing, then leaped up silently after her.

She had vanished.

The corridor opened on just two apartment doors. There were no names on either door. He smelled heavy Bavarian cooking outside one, and chose the other flat as his best bet and rang the bell.

A long time went by, and he wondered about a back exit when he heard a girl's high heels tentatively approach the door. It was opened a crack. He spoke quickly.

"Fräulein Steigmann, let me in."

She gasped and tried to slam the door shut, but he drove his shoulder hard against it. The door chain burst from its screws, and he lunged inside, pushing the girl backward, and shut and locked the door behind him. His voice was quiet.

"Please do not be alarmed, fräulein. You must have been expecting me, right?"

"I do not know you," she whispered in English.

"Call Miss Bainbury out here, please."

"But I do not understand—"

"Quickly. It's important."

She was not a very good liar; her eyes flickered to a bedroom door at one side of the room. But he let it go. "Didn't Carole Bainbury tell you to expect me, fräulein?"

"Are you—are you the man called Sam Durell? You are American, but—"

"I'm Durell. And you can relax. Bellau knows nothing about this. I think you were right to get away from the *Schloss*, fräulein. It was dangerous for you there. And it's

27

better for you and me to discuss your father privately, as well as the murder of that man this morning."

Her face was white. "But I did *not* kill Dorpler—"

"*Bitte*, Fräulein Steigmann. Now, please sit down and be comfortable. You are not my prisoner. But a certain frankness may speed us both on our way. May I have some coffee?"

There was a porcelain coffee service set on a tray before the overstuffed couch. The apartment was filled with cheap Bavarian bric-a-brac, with heavy chairs and thick lace curtains over the windows to hide the basic third-rate effect.

The girl was under a severe strain. Not more than twenty-two, she wore her thick, wheaten hair severely pulled back from a smooth, round forehead. Her full lips trembled with either fear, anger, or both. She wore a woolen gray skirt that hugged her round, Nordic hips lovingly, and her severe masculine shirt only made her carriage more provocative. Her only jewelry was an enameled pin on the shirt pocket and a practical wristwatch. He thought there might be a wild and passionate nature under her outward severity; her luminous gray eyes were articulate, filled with fleeting meanings as changeable as the clouds drifting over the Bavarian Alps. Her hands, which were strong and sensitive, trembled as she poured Durell's coffee.

"You must forgive me," she murmured. "I have had some bad, frightening days. The man, Dorpler, terrified me this morning. So I came here—it is a friend's apartment, she's gone to Switzerland for a holiday. As for Carole Bainbury . . ."

Durell did not look at the closed bedroom door. "We'll discuss her later. I can guess it was Miss Bainbury who first approached you about your father's visit here, am I right?"

She nodded, moistened her lips, folded her hands.

Durell said: "First, I want to know about Hans Dorpler and what happened at the *Schloss* this morning."

"He was terrible," Lisl whispered. "First he claimed I must help him because he aided my father to escape from the war-criminal tribunal. When I refused and said my father deserved any punishment decided for him, he grew abusive. He was beside himself. He said he was betrayed."

"By whom?"

"He was not clear. He spoke only of 'they.' "

"Was it a kind of underground outfit, say, to spirit suspected Nazis out to South America, or the Middle East?"

The girl regarded him with level eyes. "There are rumors

among people like Dorpler that such an organization exists. Dorpler said he had worked for 'them' before. But he mostly raved about the injustices done to Germany and how my father deserved medals rather than prison." Lisl shuddered. "Dorpler was a coarse, brutal man. I refused to give him money or to hide him."

"Lisl, why not? Didn't you love your father and want to see him safely back in the States?"

She made a thin sound of hate. "I was shocked to learn he still lived, when he flew secretly to Munich. He said he came only because he loved me and wanted to see me. But how can I carry such a monster's blood in my veins? I can never feel clean again." The girl paused. "But am I a monster, too, to deny my father and wish him dead?"

"Didn't he protest his innocence?"

"Of course. But don't they all?"

"What did he say in his own defense?"

She dropped her gaze from his and twisted her fingers together. "What could he say, after all?"

"Did you give him a chance?"

She trembled with anger. "Oh, you Americans are so self-righteous! Of course, he could not explain his past! He may have tried, but—I refused to listen."

Durell sipped his coffee. It was strong and bitter. He looked big and dark in the antique chair, his eyes saturnine as he regarded Lisl's nervous pacing. Her young face, so clean and wholesome, was suddenly stricken by doubt as she turned back to him.

"Was I wrong?" she whispered. Her eyes were wide. "Should I have listened? Do you think my father might be innocent?"

"We can find out," he said quietly.

"But if you are right, I have been so cruel, so unjust . . ."

He did not want to push her too far. He changed the subject. "Tell me how Dorpler fell from your window."

"Oh, he was like a wild animal. I threatened him with a gun when he demanded that I hide him. He backed to the open window and lost his balance—"

"Where is the gun?"

"He—he took it from me. It should be on—on his body." She bit her ripe, full underlip. "Please understand, my father was guilty, and I would not help him. A trial, surely, would determine that—"

29

"Lisl, why did your father come here at all, knowing how you felt about him?"

"But he did not know. I thought he was long dead. But his first words referred to a letter he said he'd had from me, asking him to come to see me if he had an opportunity."

"And did you write that letter?"

"No."

"Did he show you this letter?"

"No."

"Then he was lured here by a false note, supposedly written by you, is that it?"

She said dubiously: "It seems to be so."

"Then Dorpler helped him escape from his police cell, after you denounced him; and Dorpler worked for some 'organization' that would smuggle your father out of Germany?"

"Dorpler implied this, yes."

"But he told you nothing about such an organization?"

"Nothing." She was perplexed, and watched Durell rise smoothly from his chair. "What is it?"

"Lisl, you denounced your father to the authorities, convinced he was guilty of war crimes, even though he had just arisen from the dead, so to speak. Who put these ideas into your head? Who suggested his guilt, and who told you about it? Was it your friend, Miss Bainbury, in the next room?"

"But I trust Carole—!"

The girl looked desperate, chagrined. Durell was careful. He did not know which way she might jump, and he took no chances when he moved to the closed bedroom door. Lisl put out a hand as if to stop him, then shrugged helplessly. Durell yanked open the door.

"Come out here, Miss Bainbury."

The English girl in the bedroom, who had shadowed him since his arrival in Munich, was ready and waiting.

She held a gun, pointed at his belly.

Chapter Six

AT CLOSE range, there was nothing studious or ordinary about Carole Bainbury. It was a day for disturbed women, he thought wryly. Carole was more mature than Lisl, but she was equally apprehensive. She handled her wartime Beretta nervously, and he held out his hand for it."

"Don't be alarmed, please," he said quietly. "We both want Dr. Hubertus Steigmann, it seems, and we can decide how to share him when we're successful. Surely we can cooperate until we catch our fox, Miss Bainbury."

She hesitated, then lowered her gun with a quick, hard smile. She had abandoned her heavy glasses, and her brown hair now swung at shoulder length, instead of being done in the prim bun she had affected before. She had a deep, husky voice.

"Yes, it is as you say, Mr. Durell. First we must catch our fox. And to do that, we must find his trail. I thought I might manage it myself, but perhaps this talk is best."

"How long have you known Lisl?"

"Oh, a month or two."

"Were you at the *Schloss* this morning when Dorpler came to ask her for help?"

"No. It was all a terrible error. We wanted Hans Dorpler ourselves. He was worth something, alive, for any information he might have. Unfortunately—" She paused and gave him a brilliant smile. "When Lisl phoned me about it, I told her to come here, where I could help her. Aside from the wasted opportunity, however, Dorpler deserved to die."

"And Dr. Steigmann?"

She looked at Lisl. "He was a criminal, and it was only right that he should be arrested and tried for his crimes."

"Did you write the letter in Lisl's name that lured him here to Germany?"

Carole crossed the room to pour herself a cup of coffee. Her hands were steady now. Lisl regarded her with wide, confused eyes. She looked as if she wanted to appeal to the older woman for an explanation, but she bit her lip again

31

and was silent. Carole Bainbury's brown eyes were mocking and intelligent as she swung about to regard Durell.

"I have not been completely frank, of course. Who is, in this world? In *our* world, Mr. Durell. We are not enemies, you and I. And I had no wish to hurt Lisl, either. But I had to use her. Her father is the target for a number of international agencies who would like to brainwash him for his laser techniques—the popular 'death ray,' according to the sensational press. But I am not from the GRU, the Soviet military intelligence, nor the KGB. Neither am I working for the British M. I. 6 department, Mr. Durell." She shot an amused glance at his tall figure. "Our first objective was to lure Dr. Steigmann within reach—here, in Germany."

Lisl's voice trembled. "And then you had me betray him, to have him arrested and to stand trial?"

"Arrested, my dear, yes. Trial—no."

"You planned his escape?"

"Dear Lisl, your father's 'escape' was inevitable. Many sympathizers like Hans Dorpler were glad to help him. And many others would have done so, in order to get him to work on their side."

Durell said coldly: "And what went wrong?"

"We wanted, and expected, Steigmann to be 'rescued.' But he was only bait. We want the people who hired Dorpler to help him get away. We have been on this hunt for some time. But Dorpler is dead. Don't blame yourself, Lisl. He would have been killed by his employers, anyway, to insure his silence after his task was done. He was not very reliable."

"So you used Steigmann mainly to get a line on an underground organization that smuggles brains out of Germany?"

"From anywhere in the world," she said flatly.

"And did you get such a line?"

"We did," said Carole Bainbury. "At least, we know the name of the outfit. They call themselves the Cairo Dancers."

Chapter Seven

"GO ON," Durell said.

"But that is all we know," she insisted. "Only the name."

" 'We?' " he asked.

She was silent. Durell searched his memory, but the term she had used meant nothing to him. Nowhere in the files he had examined had he come upon the slightest hint of anything called the Cairo Dancers. It was something new and, to judge from the girl's drawn face, something very deadly. And it was what he had been looking for.

He signaled the two girls to remain where they were and moved to the telephone that stood on an ornate piecrust table near the lace-curtained window. Beyond the window was an areaway, dimly seen through the curtains, and the windows of other apartments in the same shabby building.

The back of his neck prickled with tension. He called Henry Gordon's number and listened to the telephone ring four times before Gordon replied. He sounded far away, a poor connection.

"Hank? Durell here."

"Good. Got her?"

"Both of them."

The telephone clicked rapidly.

Durell said: "Are you being bugged, Hank?"

"Not that I know of. It might be Bellau, though."

"All right. What did he report?"

"Not too much. Bellau is cooperating nicely. The medical report on Dorpler shows no knife or gun wounds, only the damage to be expected by a fall from Lisl's window at the *Schloss*. No sign of violence before his fall, but his eyes show the effects of drugs, so far unidentified, and a state of abnormal excitement. So his faculties might have been impaired."

"No word on Steigmann?"

"Bellau thinks he might still be in Munich. So far as we know, the subject hasn't left the country. Every road, train, bus and airline has been double-checked. Bellau is giving out to the press that Dorpler committed suicide, by the way —out of remorse for shaming the German people by letting Steigmann escape. Maybe it's best. But listen, Sam, I think I'm on to something—"

Durell said sharply: "Bottle it up, if the phone is tapped. We can't trust anyone. Can it wait for an hour?"

"I suppose so. Meet me at location four, can you?"

It was the code name for the Deutsches Science Museum. Durell said: "Fine, Hank. Ring off now—"

He started to hang up. As he did so, the window imploded with a crash of glass; the heavy curtains belled around

33

him, and a bullet sang like a spiteful bee into the room.

One of the girls cried out, a thin sound of pained surprise, and he saw from the corner of his eye a shade being yanked down in one of the opposite apartments. Glass had showered about his shoulders and crunched underfoot as he whirled. At the same moment, the door which he'd broken the chain of suddenly slammed inward, bouncing against the wall with a crash that brought down a heavy print. A shadow loomed there, dark and ominous. Its silhouette was accented by the quick tongues of muzzle flame from a silenced auto-pistol. The room seemed to blow apart in a cloud of shattered plaster; there was a ringing and clanging as a brass lamp hurtled across the floor. Durell's gun was in his hand. He squeezed off three shots.

There was no time to think about it.

The man in the doorway pitched back, his gun spitting flame. Durell jumped past the frozen girls and saw the enemy's face with two small, black holes in the forehead where his shots had gone true. He swore and dragged the would-be assassin inside, then toed the door shut and straightened. His breath came lightly, quickly. The room was filled with a white fog from the blasted wall plaster. His throat was dry. It had been a near one, a fast and accurate two-pronged attempt to eliminate him.

Or maybe they had tried for the girls.

Downstairs, a man shouted in hoarse, alarmed inquiry. Durell looked at Lisl and Carole.

"Are you both all right?"

Lisl nodded. Her young face was pale. But Carole Bainbury held her side tightly and said: "I've been hit. It was the first bullet that did it."

"Can you walk?"

She was calm. "I think so."

"Then let's get out. We're sitting quail here."

He took a moment to fan the dead man's pockets. The face was just a face, swarthy, fleshy-lipped, with black eyes already glazing in the death-stare of universal surprise. There was no identification. The machine-pistol was German.

"Keep down," Durell said. "The sniper is just across the areaway."

The girls crouched and watched him with wide eyes. They might have been sisters, in their communion of terror. But Carole was the calmer of the two, despite her wound.

"Who is he?" she whispered.

34

"Don't know. Algerian? One of the Dancers? An Egyptian, maybe."

Carole nodded emphatically. "Egyptian. He must be."

"Well, he's in no condition to tell us. Let's go."

There was confused shouting from the apartments below. Durell eased the door open again, stepping over the dead man. No one was in sight. He signaled the girls to follow. A back stairway led them swiftly to the ground floor. Dim whistles sounded in the street now. The danger lay in the back alley. The sniper might be waiting there, guessing their path of escape. But no shots were fired as he stepped into the warm afternoon air. Sunlight lay in buttery slabs between the old houses. Traffic glittered beyond the end of the narrow back street.

"Carole?"

"I'm all right. I can follow you."

She had courage, he decided. He saw blood on her tweed suit, under her tightly clasped arms. He nodded to Lisl to stand by her and then walked carefully to the busy corner and arranged for a taxi to take them to the Bayerischer Hof, his hotel.

He took a few precious seconds to pick up a bottle of brandy from the bar near the lobby, and as soon as he had locked the door of his room, he filled a glass for Carole.

"Drink this down. All of it. Then we'll have a look at your wound."

Surprisingly, she blushed. "But I couldn't—"

"It's no time for modesty," he said. "Lisl, you've had some training. You can help."

Lisl nodded and swallowed and watched him with big eyes as he made Carole Bainbury lie down on his bed. He worked swiftly and with some experience, easing off her blouse and then her pink brassiere. The left cup was filled with blood that oozed from the bullet wound. Her breasts were firm and provocative, rising with her quick breath as he searched for signs that the bullet might have gone into her rib cage. But the damage, though jagged, was only a shallow trough across the swelling top of her breast, bleeding copiously but hardly dangerous. He felt relieved. Lisl tore bandages from the bedsheet and murmured about antiseptics.

"We'll get a doctor later," he said. "One who won't report this to the police."

While Lisl swiftly turned professional to bandage the wound

he tried Henry Gordon on the telephone. There was no answer. He let it ring for some time, then took a brandy for himself and gave another to Lisl, who refused. Then he wondered if he should try Gordon again. It seemed warm in the hotel room. As he turned away from the bed, his toe prodded Carole's big leather bag. He was surprised that she'd had the presence of mind to take it with her. Then he saw her fine tawny eyes widen as he picked it up, and he opened it over her quickly murmured protests.

There was the usual feminine paraphernalia: a gold lipstick, tissues, powder case, British passport, change in various national currencies—mostly German—a few British half crowns and two Israeli pound notes. A curious smile of resignation moved her mouth. Her hair was disheveled, and a thin sheen of sweat made her face gleam.

"Please, I also have some aspirin in there."

She was calm, and she had an unusual combination of courage and intellect. Yet he had the feeling she did not belong in his business, and was not truly a part of it. For all that, he liked her, and felt a kinship that was disturbing. He met her eyes with a level stare.

"I think it's time you told me about your associates, Carole. You certainly don't work alone, do you?"

"No."

"Tell me who your friends are."

"I can't tell you that now. Not yet."

He searched further in her bag, opened the wallet, found an international driver's license, a letter of introduction from London that fitted Gordon's information about her, and then he discovered a small snapshot in a side pouch. Carole made a sudden effort to snatch it from him, but he held it back and studied it.

It was a desert view of what seemed to be an archaeological dig, a bleak and harsh landscape with a wadi in the background and an uncovered, ruined stone dike over the dry watercourse. Tents made black pyramids against the glaring landscape, and he recognized the tents as those of Bedouin laborers. Two figures were prominent in the foreground. One was Carole, in riding breeches and boots and a man's white shirt.

The man whose shirt she apparently wore stood with his arm possessively about her shoulders.

Durell looked long at the man's dim face and heard the girl sigh softly, and then she spoke in resignation.

36

"Do you recognize him?"

"I've seen his picture before," Durell said. "In our counterintelligence files. Yes, I know him." He looked at Carole with new respect. "His name is Simon Asche."

"That's right. That's Simon."

Something in her voice, a tone of quiet possession and a deeply satisfied warmth in her brown eyes, made Durell look up at her with quick appreciation. Simon Asche was a dangerous man. On the one hand, he was known in the business to be as elusive as a wraith, as insubstantial as smoke; on the other, he was quick, deadly, implacable. Men who had known him, in Durell's business, described him as a dark scowl, a flash of white teeth, solemn black eyes, a sensitive turn of the head. He had been a brilliant desert fighter in Israel, with the rank of a major, and it was said that he had participated in the coup that captured Nasser during the war for independence there, and then agreed to the gallant gesture that granted the Egyptians their parole and set them free. In the K Section files, which Durell was committed to study regularly, Major Asche was described as a burly, hairy-chested former Englishman who had been a heavyweight on the Oxford wrestling team. He was a brilliant scholar, adept at translating ancient scrolls in Aramaic, Egyptian hieroglyphics, classic Hebrew or Attic Greek. After his military service, Asche had returned to his true love, which was archaeology. One notation that Durell remembered in the NSA files was to the effect that Major Asche was currently at work on a dig in the Negev, exploring old Nabatean ruins. The last note stated that Asche was a member of the Shin-bet-Israeli Intelligence Service.

He replaced the faded snapshot in Carole's bag and met her calm eyes. Some of the color had returned to her cheeks, and she sat up carefully, with Lisl's help. Lisl gave her a Gauloise. The scratch of the match was abnormally loud in the stillness as Carole lit the cigarette.

"How long have you known Asche?" Durell asked.

"Simon? A lifetime—yet only moments." Her smile mocked him, but when she used his name, she looked more than lovely. "Simon wanted me to spot you and let you know it, of course. Was I appropriately clumsy?"

"You were fine. How is he, these days?"

"Devoted to his work."

"His archaeology, or espionage?"

"Simon does what he must, what any man of good conscience must do. If there are monsters in the world, he hunts for them. He heard you were being sent here. He hopes you will work with us."

She sat up on the bed and swung her legs carefully to the floor, and drew a cautious breath against her wound. She was a lovely, composed girl, intelligent and attractive. She would be efficient at her work, Durell thought, whether it was in Munich or in a desert camp. It was quiet and remote in the hotel room. The only sounds came from the traffic below.

"Suppose you tell me," he suggested, "what you don't feel free to tell Inspector Bellau."

"Do you trust Bellau?"

"He has his job to do, and that includes every effort to preserve West Germany's reformed image. But I don't trust him any more than I can trust you—or Major Asche."

"Can you divorce yourself from your conscience?" she asked.

"My job is to find Dr. Steigmann—or find where he's been taken. Is it your conscience, Carole, that made a spy out of you? Or was it because you seem to have fallen in love with the legendary Major Asche?"

"Simon is no legend," she said quickly. "No more than you are. Since you insist on an answer, I do love him. Highly unprofessional, isn't it? I should be fired from the job, because I allow emotion to be mixed with business. It makes me unreliable, in your eyes, doesn't it?"

"That depends," he said.

"And he cares for me. But he doesn't let it interfere with the work he has to do. Simon is a wonderful, sensitive man. I wish sometimes he would look at me as a woman, instead of as a professional associate, either at the dig or on missions like these. I first met him when we worked together at exploring ancient Nabatean ruins in the Negev. The land was once rich and flowering, flowing with the Biblical milk and honey, did you know that? The Nabateans used canals and irrigation systems as efficient as any we could build today. We dig with a purpose, Simon says, to make the desert bloom again. . . ."

She paused. Her brown eyes were abruptly sad and sympathetic, as she regarded Durell's tall figure. "You never allow yourself such luxuries as emotion or ideals, do you? Is it just a job to you, a contract you fulfill, a piece of work, and no more?" She halted again and looked contrite. "I'm sorry. That wasn't fair of me. And yet I wish there was something in your face that let me know I could reach you."

Lisl broke in harshly. "Herr Durell has nothing there. He is a machine only, nothing more. I think he accepts pain for himself as easily as he inflicts it on others."

Durell did not look at the younger girl. He said to Carole: "According to our records, Major Asche was recently in South America, hunting down a former SS general named Rudolph Gruningen. Were you with Asche then, too? And did you 'persuade' Gruningen to put a bullet through his brain?"

"It was a necessary job. Just as we feel it is necessary to track down Dr. Steigmann. So we are here. But we are not doing as well here as in Argentina."

He said quietly: "Because of the Cairo Dancers?"

She considered her cigarette, held somewhat awkwardly between her square fingertips. "We have the same purpose in mind; there is no reason not to share information. The strange thing about this underground railway is that the people they smuggle away just—disappear. They don't show up working for one side or the other, East or West." She paused. "Have you ever heard of a man named Colonel Selim El-Raschid? It's a cover name, we think. We don't know who or what he is. A Syrian national, originally, but an extreme pan-Arabist responsible for several revolutions in the Middle East. He was once accused of trying a coup against Nasser, too. He's a fanatic and a monster, and at the moment, El-Raschid has Dr. Steigmann."

"To what purpose?"

"To smuggle him away somewhere. To a place where he and his Dancers rule. We just don't know. But Simon says it's to force from Steigmann everything he knows about American laser developments."

"Is this Selim El-Raschid in Munich?"

"Simon thinks so. I will not deceive you. We want Steigmann, of course, if he is a former war criminal. But much more, we must smash the Cairo Dancers before something awful happens to all of us."

Chapter Eight

HE LEFT the girls in the hotel room when he went to meet Henry Gordon at the Deutsches Science Museum. They promised to wait for his return and to admit no one to the room under any circumstances. But he didn't know if he could trust either of them.

Lisl accompanied him to the door. Her young eyes searched his with confused anxiety, and she pitched her voice in a low whisper, so Carole could not overhear.

"Bitte," she said. "I owe you a debt of thanks. Perhaps I was too cruel when I said you had no emotions. I may be wrong. But I thought I saw everything clearly, and now you have made me doubt it all. I may have made a terrible mistake. But first—shouldn't I go to Inspector Bellau, instead of hiding here, and tell him all I can about Dorpler's death?"

"I'll take care of that."

"But what will happen to me now?"

"For the moment, I only want to keep you safe," he assured her. "Everything will be all right."

She shook her head, and her pale hair swung about her straight shoulders. "No, I think not. Nothing will ever be the same for me again. Was I wrong to betray my father? Carole suggested it, but—is he really guilty of all the terrible things they say he did during the Nazi regime? When I think of it now, when he first came to me, he—he seemed so lost and frightened. Was I wrong? It all happened so long ago, before I grew up, and now it seems far away, as if those days could never have been."

"It happened," he said grimly.

"But you are not sure my father is guilty?"

"I'm not sure," he said.

"But what am I to think?" she asked desperately.

"I can't tell you yet, Lisl. We'll just have to wait and see." He was impatient to go, but the girl's eyes were helpless and appealing. She touched his face with a wandering fingertip. "I think you may be a good man, after all. I do not understand the life you lead, as Carole does. You may be cruel, but I think you can be good, too, and I trust you. I need someone to help me and advise me."

"Stay with Carole," he suggested. "I think it may turn out all right."

"I want to see my father again, you understand? I want another chance to listen to him. I never let him speak out, and now I cannot rest until I am sure about him, one way or another. It is you who gave me doubts about his guilt, you see. Will you take me with you, to find him?"

"I don't know if I can. But I'll try."

"Thank you so much," she whispered.

He was surprised when she stood on tiptoe for a brief instant to brush her lips against his. Her mouth was fresh and young and wholesome. He felt a brief pang of guilt, recalling General McFee's orders, back in Washington. Aside from tracing down the missing scientists such as Dr. Nardinocchi and Professor Novotnik—ride the underground railway to its end, McFee had said—he had to find Lisl's father and take him home—or kill him.

He touched the girl's shoulder briefly, in what he hoped was some kind of reassurance, and waited until he heard her throw the bolt after he closed the door. Then he left.

The afternoon had turned abruptly chilly, and an overcast that hid the Alps threatened imminent rain. He was late for his meeting with Henry Gordon, and traffic to the Isar bridges was congested, delaying him another ten minutes. The rain began to fall, dimpling the gray river with its barge traffic. The monumental mass of the Deutsches Science Museum gleamed with lights in the quick gloom that obscured the city.

The place where he was to find Hank Gordon was near the model exhibits, those intricately operating miniature mines, industrial plants and oil refineries whose push-button controls and perfect mechanization amazed and delighted the visitors.

But Henry Gordon was not there.

He scanned the crowd rapidly, but the pleasant, bald man was not in sight. Worry began to nag at him. He did not linger too long; he did not want to be spotted. And after five minutes he walked out to the main entrance of the museum and turned up his collar against the cold rain that seemed to have settled in for the rest of the afternoon.

The science exhibits turned his mind grimly to Dr. Hu-

41

bertus Steigmann's specialty—the laser beams. He knew little more than the average reader of popular scientific journals, but it was enough to cause a deep dread in the pit of his stomach at the loss of Steigmann's information to the West.

Laser was an acronym to describe what was termed "light amplification by stimulated emission of radiation." The term rhymed with "blazer." And indeed it blazed a trail into new wonders for the world, if properly employed. The device could level beams at a medical patient's head to destroy tumors behind the eye, or bounce light off the dark side of the moon in two and a half seconds, or destroy cancers in laboratory animals, or burn a hole through the hardest diamond. The machine was both a potential miracle tool and an annihilator that might one day destroy ICBM missiles in flight or, if fired from earth-orbiting satellites, wipe out whole cities. It was controlled light, using synthetic ruby lenses to tame its electrons and create a concentrated beam that could destroy anything in its path, instantaneously. It was compact and convenient; but as far as Durell knew, the power needed to operate the device was still too great to be practicable. But he did not know what Steigmann had achieved, and it could mean one more item of terror added to the precarious balance of peace in the world.

In the hands of an amoral, power-hungry madman, the machine could tip the scales toward ultimate destruction.

"Durell?"

His reflections, as he paused in the museum doorway, were abruptly cut off by the quiet voice behind him.

He turned with his hand on the gun in his pocket and saw Major Simon Asche smiling at him.

There was iron in the man's thick black hair, and deep furrows in his craggy face, as if time had acted like erosive streams in his desert-hardened features. His black eyes snapped with amused intelligence and tough purpose; his chunky wrestler's physique looked too big for the raincoat that was stretched tight across his thick shoulders. He held out a square hand and Durell took it carefully. Simon Asche had a firm, hard grip. There was a question in the man's glance, a search, and a brief, hard challenge. Then he smiled again.

"Henry Gordon will be along soon," he said. He had a crisp British accent. "He was delayed by an accident. A truck turned over and blocked traffic. He wasn't hurt. It seemed like a legitimate accident. I thought I'd come on ahead, since we had to meet, sooner or later."

"You didn't arrange for his delay?" Durell asked.

"No. You'll have to take my word for it, though. I assume we're going to work together, unless you feel we're too far apart."

"That remains to be seen. Gordon didn't tell you of this meet."

"We tapped his phone. We heard you make the appointment. Don't be surprised, Durell. We've been set up here for some time, and we can be reasonably efficient." Asche looked at him with suddenly anxious black eyes. "I heard of the little set-to in Lisl Steigmann's apartment. Is Carole all right?"

"Wounded. It's superficial."

"I appreciate the help you gave her. She should be along any moment. I sent word to your hotel that she should join us here." Asche paused. "A council of war, so to speak."

"Not smart," Durell said sharply. "She's a prime target. She was safe in my room. Why didn't you—"

"I need her here," Asche said.

"At the risk of her life?"

Asche sighed. "We all risk our lives, don't we? Every moment of every day."

"I thought you and Carole—"

"Yes," Asche said. "But you and I know that our personal affairs count for little in our jobs. It isn't easy. I know all about you, Durell—just as I'm sure you know all about me. I think we can be friends and work together." The chunky man paused. "Besides, Carole said she'd learned something she hadn't been ready to tell you. I asked her to come along with it and meet us here."

Alarm had crystallized in Durell, clanging with the warning clamor of fire bells. "What sort of car does she use?"

"A black Porsche—"

"Let's look for it."

He turned and walked with a long stride across the rainy concrete of the parking lots by the massive museum. Asche thrust his fists in his raincoat pockets, hunched his shoulders, and followed. Durell's first impression of the man had been favorable—Asche was intelligent, tough, resourceful. His dossier proved all this. But he preferred to make his own judgment, and at the moment he had a premonition of complete disaster. . . .

"There," Asche said. "There she is."

43

He pointed to a small black Porsche parked in an official slot in a little cul-de-sac formed by the high façade of the museum. The major's voice had changed, however, catching some of Durell's tight apprehension. A troop of children splashed through puddles in a long line ahead, shepherded by a stout stern-faced woman. Their voices rang out high and clear and innocent against the sullen hiss of the rain. Pigeons waddled for shelter from the downpour, their red eyes unperturbed by the shrill sounds.

"Hold it," Durell said.

His voice abruptly halted the other man. "What is it? What's the matter?"

"I don't know."

"She's sitting in the car—"

"Stay here, Simon."

He scanned the windows of the high museum wall, his eyes searching the line of the roof, the rainy parking lot and the glistening rows of cars in the distance behind them. The back of his neck tingled. Simon Asche started forward again, only to be checked by a strong thrust of Durell's arm.

"I'll go first."

"But Carole—"

"I'm sorry," Durell said.

He knew that Asche was only too aware of the risks they took in their business. Asche was a professional, like himself. But Carole Bainbury did not know all the dirty tricks of the trade.

He had left her only a few minutes ago in the safety of his hotel room. She had been warned not to leave. But she had chosen the risk of following Asche's orders.

She sat quietly, her hands still on the wheel of the little Porsche, her brown eyes staring at the blank building wall beyond the front of the car. But she had been butchered as neatly and efficiently as a lamb in a slaughterhouse.

Her throat was cut from ear to ear.

Chapter Nine

SIMON ASCHE pushed toward the car, but Durell checked him. "Stand back, Major. You don't want to see her now."

44

The man's voice trembled. "Carole?"

"She's dead. It's a mess."

"Carole?"

His voice was strained, incredulous. Durell slammed the car door shut and pushed him back. It was like trying to move a concrete post. Simon's eyes looked blind. His harsh mouth opened and closed, his broad chest heaved convulsively.

"We—we planned to marry—when this was finished."

"Don't look at her," Durell repeated.

Simon turned his head away and stared across the rain-swept parking lot. People were running for the cars, moving like puppets jerked about on strings. The pigeons still waddled about, unconcerned by the puddles of water. The sound of children's voices was high and innocent in the distance. Simon began to tremble. Durell flexed his fist and Simon caught the gesture and shook his head sharply.

"No. I'll be all right."

"Are you sure?"

Simon nodded. "She was innocent—she worked in this just for me, you know? We were thinking of marriage—"

"Cut it out," Durell said harshly.

"The Dancers did it—those fanatic devils—"

"You'll have to tell me all about it, Simon."

"Yes. Yes, I will. . . . Will you help me?"

"I intend to. All I can."

A car swept in a wide circle around the museum lot, spraying water in thick sheets from the puddles, then rocked to a halt beside them. It was Henry Gordon. His face was pale and angry, and he dashed the back of his hand against his heavy moustache. Durell let Gordon look in the Porsche at Carole Bainbury's piteous body. Gordon made a sound in his throat and turned in anger to Simon.

"Why didn't you order her to cooperate with us?"

"Shut up," Durell said. "It's bad enough for him."

"But she held out on you, you know, in your hotel. She was saving some items for Simon."

Simon Asche said flatly: "My fault. An error of judgment. I wasn't sure you would work with us. If only I'd told her—"

Durell said to Gordon: "We haven't much time here. What did Carole have?"

Gordon drew a deep breath. "Two things. Quite useful, too. She hid the stuff in your bed, while you attended to her

45

wound. Not your fault, Cajun. You were distracted for the moment. She told Lisl about it after you left, and she decided to follow you. Lisl gave the stuff to me after Carole insisted on leaving your room."

"Let's have it," Durell said.

Gordon dug in his coat pockets and produced a postcard and what looked like an admission ticket and handed them to Durell, keeping a careful eye on the stunned Simon Asche. Simon made no objection.

"Watch him," Durell said to Gordon.

Simon said harshly: "I'm all right."

"You only think so."

He considered the two items Gordon handed him. There seemed no connection between them. The postcard was a typical museum souvenir purchase from Munich's Alte Pinakothek, the art museum. It was a reproduction of an eighth-century Byzantine mosaic, depicting a cassocked monk with round head uplifted, one foot raised, and arms lifted in a high plea for benediction. The posture was peculiar. The monk seemed to be dancing, transfixed by an inner sense of beatitude that was unusual for the subject.

The second item, the ticket, was a small pasteboard granting one admission to the *Oktoberfest*—that famous fair that was a lusty Bavarian kaleidoscope of rump-slapping folk dances, thumping brass bands, and enormous beer halls.

Durell pocketed the postcard and the ticket and kept his face blank. "Gordon, did you get a good look at the truck that blocked traffic and kept you from getting here?"

The CIA man pushed rain from his moustache with a white knuckle. "It was from one of the entertainment troupes putting on a show at the *Oktoberfest*."

"Good enough," Durell said.

"It ties in?"

"Why not? Did you see any name on the truck?"

"It was a local concern. But there was theatrical gear and a lot of people crammed aboard."

"Check. Now what about Lisl?"

"Behind your locked and bolted door. I think I scared her enough to keep her safe for you there, Sam."

The windows of the great museum glowed with light against the gathering dusk. The rain was now a steady drizzle that seemed to have settled in for the rest of the evening. Durell drew a deep breath. He did not allow himself to think too much about Carole's death, and the way it

46

had been accomplished, but he felt a burden of responsibility for it which was almost as great as Simon's. If the girl had obeyed him, she might still be alive. But in his business there was no profit in crying over the proverbial spilt milk. He could see that Simon knew this, too, but he could only guess at the inner agony the other man suffered. The lines in Simon's face had deepened measurably in the last moments, and he looked exhausted, as if he had spent the last of his strength in a desperate sprint that failed.

He wished he could say something to ease Simon's burden; but when he spoke, it was with a terse efficiency.

Something had to be done about the dead girl and the bloody car. Inspector Bellau had to be notified, and if possible, the event was to be kept out of the press. When he suggested this, Simon made a negative gesture; Durell rode over his hoarse protest.

"We have to let Bellau handle it. I don't trust him any more than you, but he'll cooperate on this. It's to his own advantage to keep publicity out of this. And I'll want a little time." Durell looked at his watch. "See if you can hold him off for twenty minutes."

Gordon said: "What's on your mind, Sam?"

"Something I want to do alone."

"I'm going with you," Simon announced. "If you have an idea where these people can be found—"

"Later. You won't be left out of the kill, Simon."

"Not for a moment. Not now, not later," the man said harshly. "I want my hands on the man who did this to Carole."

"Then obey orders, and we'll make it. Go off half-cocked, and the same thing may happen to you." Durell's voice was low and flat. "We're not dealing with amateurs. Neither are they professionals as we understand it. I think we're up against a crew of fanatics who place absolutely no value on human life, neither ours nor theirs. Understand?"

"But I—"

"You keep Lisl Steigmann safe. That's of first importance. We'll meet later at my hotel—if I'm lucky."

He told them to wait until after ten o'clock that night, once they were finished with Bellau. He would see them then.

But Durell had no wish or expectation that this would happen. He hoped to buy a ticket on the ghost railway and begin his ride to its unknown terminal.

Chapter Ten

THE RAIN did not dampen the Bavarian gaiety at the *Oktoberfest* grounds. There was noise and light, the thump of bands, the glitter of advertising from competing beer halls, the blare of sound from exhibition booths, and the gaudy whirl of wild neon to make the fair resplendent. Durell wasn't sure just what he was looking for, but he knew he would recognize it when it was found.

He let himself be pushed this way and that by the red-faced, stout, and beery throngs. There was an earthy quality to the *Oktoberfest*, a bawdy joy as if the fair were a remnant of ancient pagan rites celebrated at this season of the year. He let himself drift about with the tides of surging people.

No one followed him. He did not try to hide himself, and even hoped he might spot a persistent shadow among the laughing faces that surrounded him. But he found nothing. He wished he could spot something tangible; it was always better to know the face and presence of your foe. To move into unknown shadows always wracked nerves to a point where a premature response might be triggered. It was a ticklish and uncertain coup he had to achieve, and he might be killed without a chance to manipulate his stratagem toward the goal he sought. He wanted them to take him alive and transport him along the route they had taken for Dr. Hubertus Steigmann. But they might have decided to eliminate Sam Durell, K Section agent. For them it would be the simplest and safest course. So he had to make them think he had a high enough value to them to insure his life.

It would not be easy to effect.

Even if he succeeded that far, he could face torture and bone-twisting, spiteful vengeance. He just did not know. He pushed these dour thoughts from his mind and walked on through the gay and uninhibited crowds.

He found what he wanted, soon enough.

In a way, except for the difficulty of learning their name, they operated with a brazen frankness that reflected either utter complacency or recklessness.

There was a pavilion which advertised, in bold neon meant to imitate Arabic script, *The Cairo Dancers.*

He gave it no more than a casual glance when he walked by the first time. It was a flamboyant affair of gilded domes and minarets, lit by colored floodlights that played on the flimsy plastered façade. The wail of flutes and the thud of tambours came dimly through the crowd noises around the triple Moorish arches of the entrance. The Arabic neon script fluttered brazenly above the crowd of Munichers and tourists who hoped to see fabled belly dancers and seductive houri in gauze skirts. Durell walked into an adjacent beer hall, where Bavarian brass clashed out a folk dance to the accompanying thud of ribald feet and slapping hands, then he turned and sauntered around a corner toward the back entrance of the Dancer pavilion.

He had no illusions about his safety, after the way Carole had died. Her death was brutal, and although at the time he allowed little of his shock to touch him, the image of her slaughtered body crumpled in the Porsche came back to haunt him for a moment. He shivered, paused, and went on.

Somehow, he had to persuade someone in the pavilion that he was valuable enough to be sold a ticket to somewhere. . . .

"Effendi? You wish to see performance? Main door just around corner to your left, effendi. A thousand thanks . . ."

The doorman at the back entrance was all bows and suave smiles. He understood stage-door johnnies, and that made it a little easier. Durell plucked a name he remembered off the front billboard advertising.

"I have a date with Mademoiselle Zuzu," he said, and his smile had just the right touch of self-conscious embarrassment and hope for lustful adventure that the doorman might expect from a tourist jingling coins in his pocket.

"Oh, yes, effendi. Zuzu very popular gel. Always nice to gentlemen admirers, when she feels in good mood. But fine artist, very temperamental—"

"I understand." A wad of folded currency changed hands and the fat Arab bowed and opened the door. Durell had the feeling he was being welcomed into a spider's web. "She dances now, effendi. Five, ten minutes, no more. You wait at end of hall, yes?"

"Of course. Thanks, old chap."

"A pleasure, effendi."

He went inside and the door closed behind him. The wail of Arab flutes and the offbeat clamor of skin drums and jingling bells came faintly through a confused dimness before him. There was a wide hallway onto which dressing rooms opened, cluttered with theatrical baggage, stage flats and props. From beyond the dressing-room doors came an occasional hum of girls' voices in a multilingual babble. A blonde girl who looked Scandinavian ran past him in black briefs and bra, bouncing and jiggling in her haste; he turned and asked, "Mademoiselle Zuzu?"

She stopped and turned her head toward him. She gave him a swift, piercing glance before she shook her head and slid behind one of the dressing-room doors. He moved on, reluctantly.

At the end of the corridor there was a wide stage area that paralleled the bellying curtain, beyond which the performance proceeded to the appreciative audience of fat Munich men and gaping tourists. There came a burst of sound, like a simultaneous exhalation from a hundred male throats, and the flutes shrilled to a new crescendo. The curtain waved suggestively and then the corridor was suddenly flooded with perspiring, half-naked dancing girls in glittery, spangled costumes who gushed by him in a hurried frenzy for the next act.

He turned to the stairway on the right. A squad of male dancers followed the girls offstage, clad in baggy silk pants and short, gilt-embroidered red vests straight out of The Arabian Nights. They wore short, ugly scimitars in jeweled belts, and they all looked like tough and burly characters. Durell deliberately bumped one and felt the curved blade at the fellow's hip. His thumb began to bleed. The scimitars were real, and razor-sharp—hardly a normal prop for a legitimate belly-dance troupe. He began to feel more hopeful, and at the same time felt apprehensive warnings cool the nape of his neck. He wondered which one of these tough, sweaty men might have slit Carole Bainbury's throat an hour ago.

A plump little man in a blue pinstripe business suit waved jeweled, fluttering hands before him and spoke in a falsetto voice. "No, no! Please, no entrance, effendi. You must wait outside."

"I have an appointment with Mademoiselle Zuzu."

The man sneered. "Indeed? She did not tell me."

"Does she tell you everything?"

The plump man started to reply, checked himself, and said, "One moment, please," and called something in guttural Arabic to one of the male dancers, shrilling criticism of the man's performance. Blue Pinstripe was obviously a choreographic director, to judge by his blast at the panting man. Durell's Arabic was a bit rusty, but he gathered enough of the spit of words to understand that much. He waited with just the right touch of impatient uncertainty that a man with his appointment might show. The choreographer then turned back to him with a hint of asperity and some condescension.

"Now, sir, what is it you wish?"

"I told you, I have a date with Mademoiselle Zuzu."

"So you stated. Are you quite certain of this?"

"Why shouldn't I be?"

"She did not record it with me, that is why."

"Are you the date bureau for this harem?"

The face smiled, but the eyes were like chips of black stone. "You may say so, yes, Mr.—"

"Durell," he said.

"Durell?"

"That's right."

Nothing changed in the round, brown face. "I am sorry, sir, there must have been a mistake. Zuzu sees no one tonight."

"Look, I paid good money—"

"I am sorry. The doorman will refund your bribe."

It sounded as if Blue Pinstripe meant it. No tickets were for sale—not at this wicket, Durell decided. But he could not turn back now. He knew he was in the correct station.

The upper floor seemed to be distinctly off-bounds for most of the entertainment troupe, although some of them had not been warned. Two girls, wearing scanty skirts hung on round, plump hips, their eyes brilliant with kohl, started up past Durell with sidelong, speculative glances, only to be halted by another spate of high-pitched objections from Blue Pinstripe. This time the name of El-Raschid came into play. The girls turned away promptly and, with obvious alarm, hurried off. Durell drew a long breath.

"If I cannot see Mademoiselle Zuzu—"

"You cannot, sir."

"Then I'd like a chat with Herr Doctor Hubertus Steigmann."

This time there was a momentary widening of the annoyed black eyes in the suet face. A small sound bubbled in the wattled throat. "I beg your pardon, sir?"

"I think you heard me correctly." Durell moved closer to the bulging belly. "Lead the way like a good chap, eh?"

His gun exerted just enough pressure in the soft, sexless flesh to make the plump man wince. Panic, and then a malicious pleasure came and went across the moon face.

"My employer will not like this," he said softly. "You are a very foolish man."

"Is El-Raschid here?" Durell asked.

"His Holiness is present. But no one—none of the common people—may see him. Nor will you."

"I think I will," Durell said. "Even if I have to blow a hole through your blubber to peek through."

There was a hesitation, a flicker of pink tongue across brown lips, then a slow nod. "My life is of little importance. But if you say your name is Durell—"

"It is."

"Then perhaps you are expected."

"I have no doubt," said Durell. "Up we go."

He managed to herd the man up the temporary stairs without attracting attention or raising an alarm either on-stage or in the back corridors. Music clashed, cymbals banged, and flutes began again as the next number started. The dancing girls hurriedly lined up behind the curtain, adjusting flimsy straps, jeweled belly-bands, and feathered headdresses as Durell went up the steps behind the broad, waddling rump of the man in the pinstripe suit. He did not allow himself to be distracted by the girls. His stomach tightened, and every nerve tingled.

At the head of the stairs, one of the Dancers armed with a scimitar waited for them.

"It is all right, Abdulla," said his guide. "I vouch for this American."

"His Holiness expects him?"

"It is Allah's will."

The guard stepped aside. Durell followed the dancing master down a flimsy maze of temporary corridors in the pavilion above the audience hall. The appreciative applause of the all-male spectators down there was only a dim sound, like a distant thunderclap, muffled by infinite distance. He turned one corner, then another, each seemingly more dimly lit than the other. He began to think he was meant to be the victim of a delusion act when his unwilling guide halted and sighed.

"In here, sir."

The door was just another door.

"You first," Durell suggested.

"I am not permitted such a transgression."

"You already have many sins to explain to Allah," Durell said gently. "One more will hardly matter."

The man's hands trembled with genuine fear as he opened the door. Durell put a palm flat against the broad back and shoved hard, then followed inside, took a step to the right, and put his shoulders against the wall. But the others—or perhaps it was one man, he couldn't be sure—were waiting.

Blue Pinstripe gave a feminine squawk of terror and stumbled to his knees. Durell glimpsed a primitive room framed by rough, portable partitions—windowless, with only a cot and a hard chair and an unshaded electric bulb that dangled from the ceiling. Then something slashed at his gun wrist with stunning speed, and from the tail of his eye he saw a sap descend for the back of his head. He ducked, just enough to make the blow a glancing one, but pitched forward on his face as if his knees had been knocked out from under him. He let his gun go and saw a brown hand scoop it up. There was a mutter of disdainful Arabic as the fat choreographer was ordered to get up and get out of there.

"I—I did my job well!" Pinstripe stuttered.

"Perhaps it was too easy. We will leave them alone for a moment and see, before we decide."

"D-decide what?"

"Whether or not to slit the American's throat. Now move on, and go about your work."

Durell never saw the man who clobbered him. He did not try to. It would have interfered with his act to make his stunned helplessness seem genuine. He was grateful that no one kicked him or ground a heel on his hands. But perhaps it meant that they had no use for him—as he hoped to convince them they might—and merely intended to execute him with the same despatch shown with Carole Bainbury.

When he judged the time was proper, he groaned and struggled up to a sitting position and looked at the man who cowered on the cot in the little prison cubicle.

His hunches had been right.

His first hunch was that the Dancers would be ready and waiting for him.

53

His second hunch, also turned out right on the nose, when he recognized his cellmate as Dr. Hubertus Steigmann.

Chapter Eleven

IT DID not take much acting to pretend that his head ached. It did. He groaned and swayed, observing the man who shrank back on the cot in the makeshift cell. The glare of the single overhead light was blinding. Durell allowed himself a moment, as if to get his bearings, to assess the barriers that kept him prisoner. The partitions were flimsy enough; the door might resist him, however. But one good yank on the dangling light cord would give him a weapon in the form of electric wire that could be turned swiftly into a lethal garrote. The knowledge of this reassured him. In any case, he did not wish to escape; he merely wanted to stay alive.

"You're Dr. Steigmann," he said to the man on the cot. He made his voice vague and uncertain. "Aren't you?"

The other nodded. His English was still tinged with heavy Teutonic gutturals. "I am. What have they done to you? Are you a prisoner, too?"

"It seems so."

"You made them angry, young man, and that was very foolish. These are dangerous, fanatic people." The laser expert shook his bearded head. "Are you an American agent, sent to find me? I have been expecting it to happen."

"My name is Durell—Sam Durell."

"It was hopeless. They have sent you to commit suicide."

"Well, I found you, didn't I?" Durell said loudly. He put a hint of bravado and asperity in his tone. He would have bet all his prospects of survival on the fact that listening devices were pinned to the thin walls around them. All his plans depended on it. "It wasn't too hard, Dr. Steigmann. After all, we have almost enough on this Dancers outfit to hang them from the maypole."

Dr. Hubertus Steigmann was a solid, middle-aged man with a bristle of Hindenburg iron-gray hair and large Prussian-blue eyes. He had a sensitive mouth and a neatly trimmed Van Dyke beard. His dark, double-breasted suit was rumpled and stained by what he had been through these past two or three days. There was a mottled bruise on his cheekbone that stood out sharply against the waxen pallor of his skin. His face was remarkably unlined, however. He did not move. He seemed to be a man who knew how to contain himself; his body was without motion, at rest on the cot; and yet the hands folded on his knee trembled a little.

Worst of all, Durell thought, were his eyes. They were wide and childish, when they should have been sharp with cold intelligence. They looked stunned and blinded, as if by some deep, tragic grief, reflecting a wound to the mind behind them that might be beyond repair. Steigmann stood up like a sleepwalker, then paused two paces from Durell.

"Yes, you were foolish, young man. Durell, you say? How could your people have known anything about the Dancers?"

"I'm here, aren't I? It wasn't difficult. As I said, Washington has plenty of hot dope on this outfit."

"But what can Washington know? They are diabolical, these people, a mixture of religious fanaticism and political ambition that defies prediction."

Durell hoped that his listeners were hard at work. "Oh, we have our plans," he said airily. "The crackdown is due shortly, and I don't think you and I have much to worry about. There are others coming after me, you know."

"That is good," Steigmann whispered. He nodded his bearded head once, then again, and stepped back, still facing Durell, to sit down heavily on the cot. His face was all highlight and shadow in the sharp light thrown by the ceiling bulb. Durell moved toward him and let the top of his head graze the bulb and send it swaying back and forth, to make the shadows slide crazily across the cell. "That is good," Steigmann sighed again. "But I am afraid it is too late for me."

Durell rubbed the back of his aching head. "It's never too late, Doctor. You did a fool thing, coming here to Germany to see your daughter. But we'll straighten it all out."

Something flickered in the round, stunned eyes. "You— you saw Lisl?"

"A fine girl. Very lovely."

"She detests me," Steigmann said hoarsely. "My own daughter, my little Lisl—she calls me a monster, a depraved beast."

"Well, whatever you did in the past . . ."

55

"But I did nothing! She would not let me explain!"

"All of you have explanations for the atrocities you committed," Durell said, shrugging. "Usually, you all claim you were merely obeying military orders."

"But I had nothing to do with such things! Lisl would not listen. The way she looked at me!" The bearded man suddenly buried his face in his hands, and something like a sob escaped from between his shaking fingers. "And so she denounced me to the police and spoke of me as if I were less than human—"

"You should have told her the truth," Durell said sympathetically, stabbing at the unknown.

"How could I? That would have been even worse."

"How, worse?"

Steigmann shook his head, like a wounded animal trying to shake off pain. "I cannot tell you."

"You'll have to, when we get out of here."

"We will never escape from the Dancers."

"But my people know I'm here." He could not pretend to too much naïveté, so he added: "Listen, Dr. Steigmann, they're probably getting every word we say, so we must be careful. And there isn't much time. They put us together to get information, you understand, so be careful in your replies. You know what I want. You have data on the laser beam developments; you took the stuff to London. None of my people can find it now."

"I took it with me, yes," Steigmann whispered. "It was a mistake."

"What was in the papers?" Durell asked harshly.

"Formulae, notes—just scribblings I made to illustrate some points to my London colleagues. I assure you, they will be intelligible to no one but myself."

"Only you could explain them?"

"Yes, that is so," Steigmann sighed.

"Have you been asked to interpret your formulae?"

"Not yet. But it is coming, I am sure."

"Will you do so?"

Steigmann looked up, and for the first time there was life behind his wounded, stunned eyes. "What else can I do? They offer me friendship, safety, a place where I will not be falsely accused, a place where I can work—"

"Where?"

"I do not know. It is with the Dancers."

56

Durell said angrily: "And you'll work with them? Give them all you know?"

"I have nothing left but my work, young man. If that is taken from me, I can only die."

"That could happen, too," Durell said. He did not like the drift of Steigmann's thoughts, and he had hoped to find more resistance in the man. But whatever had happened since Steigmann's denunciation by his daughter, and his arrest and escape, his morale had been undermined until he was nothing but putty in the hands of any strong-minded man who wished to manipulate him. It added complications to his job that he'd hoped he could avoid. He said: "What did your papers consist of, exactly?"

"A folder of scribbled notes. They were in my pockets when I was arrested by Inspector Bellau."

"Did he take them?"

"No. I was treated courteously and searched only for arms. I had none, of course."

"So your notes were with you when the Dancers got you?"

"Yes."

"And the Dancers have them now?"

"Yes."

"Listen, you must have more hope, you must trust me. My people know enough about the Dancers to—"

There came the interruption that he'd been expecting for the past few minutes. He did not know if his gambit had been successful. Everything he had said was designed to make his listening captors anxious to learn more about what K Section might know about the Dancers outfit. If he had won their curiosity, he might also win a respite on his own execution. But if he wasn't believed, then the man in the doorway behind him might snuff out his life with a snap of his fingers.

He turned slowly, with a smile of confidence he did not feel.

Chapter Twelve

HE KNEW at once he was facing Selim El-Raschid.

Two armed Dancers flanked the man, and these were a different breed from those who doubled as performers on the public stage below. Their glittering eyes betrayed total scorn for life, either their own or other's. They were like twin hounds, and they looked enough alike to have been identicals, as perhaps they were. They were honed to a sharp tautness, as if held in check by a steel leash. A sense of death moved into the little cell with them, like a breath of icy wind.

Big as these men were—taller than Durell, who was imposing by any standards—the figure between them was even more powerful and dynamic than his guards, shrinking them into relative insignificance. Where the guards wore European clothes of dark color, Selim El-Raschid preferred the traditional, even medieval, costumes of the ancient Caliphate. One would have thought this might give the man the look of a masquerade, but the opposite was true. The thought flickered through Durell's mind that here was a person designed to march across the stage of history with devastating effect. Everything was exaggerated in him: the hawk's face, the intelligent, almond eyes, the brown smooth skin, the powerful body that towered in egomaniacal strength. An electric aura charged the air of the room. Mighty Saladin might have looked like this, or Charlemagne, or any of half a dozen conquerors whose histories had shaken the foundations of the world.

"On your knees!" one of the guards barked. "On your knees before the Second Prophet of Allah!"

Dr. Steigmann had experience with the order, and dropped at once into an astonishing, groveling posture.

Durell remained standing.

"On your knees!" the second guard shouted.

Selim El-Raschid lifted a strong, brown hand that sparkled with jewels. "It is not necessary. He does not yet understand. It may not be seemly, but we will speak with the dog, Mahmoud."

"Holy One—"

"Be silent."

The guard fell quiet, but a trembling possessed him, and again Durell thought of a deadly hunting animal straining to have his leash slipped. He knew he had to be careful in executing the plan he had formed—more than careful. His life in the hands of these twin assassins could hang by a most delicate thread. But he remained on his feet.

Selim had a cultured, Oxonian accent. "Mr. Sam Durell, of course. Field chief for K Section of the U. S. Central Intelligence Agency, sometimes operating out of Geneva Central. On assignment to recover poor Dr. Hubertus Steigmann, and cooperating with members of the *Sherutei Betahan,* the Israeli Intelligence. You may stand, Dr. Steigmann."

Steigmann scrambled to his feet with labored breath. El-Raschid smiled gently. He had a thin black moustache that joined an elegant, small black beard. His hawk's nose was pinched at the nostrils, betraying the only emotional tension Durell could detect in him.

"You admit your identity, Mr. Durell?"

Durell shrugged. "Why not? Your hopped-up goons don't worry me as much as you think they do."

"You are brave, but your bravery may be mingled with rash stupidity. You know, of course, that we heard every word you said to the learned doctor?"

Durell took a calculated risk. He had to intrigue El-Raschid by implying he knew enough about the Dancer outfit, and that K Section was also alerted, so that El-Raschid would take him captive on the underground railroad, rather than execute him out of hand. He said casually: "I took the chance that you might have the place bugged. It makes no difference. My people know about you and we'll move when we're ready. We've handled bigger problems than you." Durell's laughter was hard. "What's all the 'Second Prophet' business? Have you designs on immortality among your followers, Mr. El-Raschid?"

His confident tone sounded hollow in his own ears. But one of the hounds stirred and leaned forward, and although he showed no weapon, there was no mistaking his yearning desire to kill Durell then and there. Again the man in the middle restrained his guard.

"What I am and what I shall become are of no moment, my dear Durell. It is what *you* are and what you may become that should concern you now. I must say, you are very close to death."

"And so are you," Durell returned. "I'm not alone in this, you know."

"You are lonelier than you think, or you would like me to believe. I am suspicious, Mr. Durell. A man in your profession should hold his tongue more carefully."

For a heart-squeezing moment, Durell felt that his gambit to make himself valuable enough to be taken captive had failed. The man was too intelligent to be fooled. He had to admit that the aura of power emanating from his opponent was greater than he had expected. This was no ordinary man, with wits and training he was prepared to counter. He'd always known that one day he might meet his equal or better; the statistics on survival in his business were always discouraging, but so far he had beaten the odds. Now, he was not so sure. He heard the gusty breathing of Dr. Steigmann behind him, and knew that the same uncertain terror gripped the bearded scientist. But he allowed none of this uncertainty to show on his face or bearing as Selim El-Raschid considered him with heavy-lidded, almost sleepy black eyes. They were reptilian eyes that weighed him without emotion.

"Yes, I am suspicious of you, Mr. Durell, and I do not underrate your abilities. I have almost as complete a dossier on you as your friends in the KGB Center in Moscow. You are neither foolish nor reckless. And this last factor persuades me that you may have information of use to me. I have been curious about your super-secret K Section for some time, and although I know much, you may fill in the few gaps that are inevitable in such gleanings. You must tell me all that K Section knows about what you call the 'Dancers.' "

"Not a chance," Durell said flatly.

"Do not be hasty. I am not a vengeful man, pandering to spite to salve my ego, yet you surely know that persuasion has no limits beyond the mortality of human flesh. The instinct to survive is too strong in a man like you to hold out against the refinements I have at hand to 'persuade' you to cooperate." El-Raschid paused, and his smile was almost benign. "Yes, I have doubts about you, Mr. Durell, and I cannot forgive you for the episode in Fräulein Lisl's apartment in Munich. You killed one of my Dancers there, and for this you must suffer due punishment and then indoctrination—if my decision is favorable to you."

"One of your Dancers also murdered Carole Bainbury," Durell said harshly.

"Yes, that was Mahmoud, here. He is a very refined instrument, quick and efficient and heartless. It was necessary to eliminate her. She and her Israeli associate, Simon Asche, were a nuisance. Just as you are." Selim El-Raschid sighed. "It would really be simpler if I left you to Mahmoud and his brother."

"What country do you really work for?" Durell asked.

The man smiled. "Am I a child to reply to such bluntness? But I do not mind. Expedience warrants your immediate removal, and yet—you *could* be useful to me, for a time. Life is precious, is it not? Every day gained, every hour

60

and minute, for example, gives hope to a man condemned to die. Each instant can be a lifetime. . . . No, I work for no country and no man except for the land of Allah Himself, praised be His name. I am His true Prophet, a second son of Allah, meant to bring light and peace to all the world. And so it shall be." Again Selim paused and smiled, his cruel brown lips parting to reveal white teeth. "I see you think I am a madman, touched by a pseudo-divine mission. Your opinion is of no importance. I do wish I could believe in your usefulness to me, Mr. Durell—"

It was time, Durell decided, to convince him.

He made his play.

The next moment was like walking a razor's edge, but it had to be risked. To persuade El-Raschid was a dangerous thing, but he had to have that ticket McFee had ordered him to purchase. One way or another, he had nothing to lose but his life.

He had the twin hounds to consider, especially Mahmoud, who seemed the most eager of the two. He needed a shield against them they would not dare to smash. And he chose Dr. Steigmann.

The two giants and El-Raschid had moved inward from the doorway. Just behind Durell was the doctor, practically breathing down his neck. His own gun was gone, but the guards had no weapons in their hands. The split-second difference would help.

He moved with flashing speed that took advantage of that momentary difference, reaching backward for Steigmann and hurling the bearded man bodily toward the trio that blocked his "escape" from the cell. Steigmann stumbled and smashed into them with a bellow of surprise and fear. But it was like throwing a pebble at a concrete pillbox. The hounds reacted smoothly by sweeping the middle-aged scientist out of their way and leaping simultaneously with a deadly flowing motion toward Durell. But Durell was not there when they converged on him. His charge took him around the two and he crashed into El-Raschid, whose great size was more than that of his twin bodyguards. El-Raschid staggered, however, and Durell chopped at his throat, swung about and kicked at the first hound nipping at his heels, felt a hand grip his sleeve and claw at the fabric as if with fingers of steel, and then he broke free.

He was through the doorway with a swift, solid rush

that carried him far down the maze of corridors toward the stage stairs before the guards took after him. They had to leap over Steigmann's sprawled figure for just the split-second's delay that Durell had hoped for. In that time Durell remembered a pair of hunting dogs that his old Grandpa Jonathan had used for game in the bayous around Peche Rouge in Louisiana—lean, hungry animals whose every instinct had been honed to murderous perfection. He knew his chances were almost too small to calculate.

He did not hesitate at the head of the stairs. Mahmoud was a few inches closer at his heels, and he could have swung about and sent the man headlong down the steps in the hope of breaking his neck. But he meant to save Mahmoud, thinking of Carole Bainbury, for a later destiny. He caught the smooth iron rail and lifted himself free of the treads and slid with sickening speed down to the stage wings, heedless of the burn on his hands. Halfway down he vaulted the rail and dropped twelve feet to the floor below.

He landed in the middle of a mass of warm, perspiring female bodies, more naked than not, as a line of the girl Dancers came offstage at the end of their act. There were screams and shrieks in half a dozen languages. He staggered, caromed off an incredibly developed brunette, felt thighs, hips and breasts in soft and clumsy resistance, and got to his feet again to plunge toward the stage. He had put the girls between himself and the hounds. But the stage would not do. Something hissed by his ear, nicking the lobe, to thud with a shimmer of steel into a wooden post webbed with stage weights and cords. He grabbed at the ropes and yanked them loose and heard satisfactory thuds and crashes behind him as he swung around the pillar and ran down the wide floor behind the bellying curtain.

He had gained a few more seconds on his pursuers. But he didn't want to get too far ahead.

He was again in the maze of cubby-like dressing-rooms that served the more outstanding performers. He left behind him a seething cauldron of yelling voices and the quick brass of an alarm bell. What the audience out front might think of the confusion didn't seem to matter. Then he saw the languorous blonde he had first spoken to when he came into the pavilion.

She was just shutting her door, staring wide-eyed at the uproar and Durell's running figure. Her mouth opened briefly, then her hand lifted to beckon him, and he swerved toward her.

"Quick! In here," she whispered.

For the moment, having turned a corner, he was out of sight of the two hounds. He dived past the girl and as she stepped back, he slammed the door shut. Panting, he leaned against it and regarded her. When she started to speak, he clapped a hand over her mouth and dragged her hard against him in a violent warning should she betray him.

But she did not resist. Her ripe body pressed hard against his, trembling at the sound of feet pounding past the door. The brazen bell clanged again. More feet ran past, and thick Arabic orders were shouted. Durell relaxed his grip slightly on the girl's waist and took his hand from her mouth.

"Thanks," he said.

"It isn't much help." She whispered in English, but her accent was definitely Scandinavian. Her costume, too, was scanty enough to prove she was a blonde. She flushed under his sweeping stare and reached for a thin robe and shrugged into it. "By the way," she said, "I'm the Mademoiselle Zuzu you were looking for. I was afraid to admit it before, because I wasn't told of an appointment with you."

"And now?"

"I don't care."

"Is there any way out of here?"

"None, I'm afraid."

The dressing-room was just a six-by-six cubicle crowded with scattered costumes, trunks, and furnished with a single chair and a stained mirror circled with make-up lights. Durell drew an unsteady breath. The girl watched him.

"Why are they after you?"

"I've offered His Holiness, the Second Prophet."

"But the twins—how horrible they are!—they will kill you if they catch you here, and they will do awful things to me, too. . . ."

"Then why offer to help me?" he asked.

"I don't know. It was an impulse. I'm beginning to regret it. I hate them, but I'm afraid of them, and that creepy Harakim—the dance master, you know?—makes passes at me. It was just an impulse," she said, sighing. "Mama always said my nature would get me into trouble this way."

He wanted to ask a score of questions, but there was no time. There was a clamor in the corridor, sweeping back this way again. Doors slammed, startling the outraged girls in the act of changing costumes, and their cries told Durell he had only moments left. Again he searched for a way out, to prolong the chase and make it look good. But he had darted into a blind alley, here in the statuesque blonde's room, and he was finished.

"Mr. Durell?" she said quietly.

He turned, wondering how she knew his name, but he was not quite quick enough. The curious twist of her smile warned him, but it was too late. Something slashed at his head, making the dressing lights explode into a dozen rainbows. But that was not the worst of it. As he fell forward in dismay, aware of her remarkable strength as she pulled him away from the door, he reluctantly chalked one up for the Dancers.

The female of the species was more dangerous.

He caught only a glimpse of shining glass and steel as she drove a hypodermic into the back of his neck. In the instant before the needle went home, he realized that his prior request to see Mademoiselle Zuzu had resulted in the girl being alerted from the spider-web center upstairs, and ordered to wait for him and trap him.

Then the needle plunged home.

He saw her smile, curiously tender, and her rich body leaned forward solicitously toward him as he whirled off into a space filled with flashes of light that abruptly dimmed and faded into a total blackout.

Chapter Thirteen

TIME AND space were confused. He could find no relationship between his body of bone and flesh and muscle and his environment. He was alternately hot and suffocating, then icy cold and shivering; his teeth rattled and his jaws ached. It did not matter. He was aware of these reactions, but they seemed to be no part of him. He felt weightless, and then knew sickening descents and risings and soarings; he heard noise he could not define. At no time could he move more than an inch or two in any direction. He could see nothing except occasional flashes of light that had no meaning. He knew he was alive and that he was being transported somewhere. That was all. He had bought his ticket and he was on his way to—somewhere.

That was victory enough.

Then came a long time when he knew nothing at all, and when it ended he felt a deep and primordial fear that had nothing to do with rational knowledge; it was something that lurched up out of his very essence and shrieked only for survival, nothing more.

He was sick when he came to, with a steady, wracking nausea that knew no end. Slowly and fuzzily, as his thoughts began to cohere and the disintegrated portions of his personality became whole again, he realized he was suffering the after-effects of the drug in Mademoiselle Zuzu's hypodermic.

The cramping ropes on his body were gone. But that made no difference, either. He had no desire to go anywhere.

As his awareness grew, he knew he had been transported a long, long way, by a variety of means—car, trains and air. But where he was at this moment remained a matter of doubt.

His neck was stiff, his head pounded, and his body was soaked in sweaty rags. When he lifted his head to look about, the reaction was so severe that he lay shivering for many minutes before he ventured to try it again. He made no sound, except for his irregular, stertorous breathing; he changed nothing in his outward aspect. Better to be thoroughly conscious, he decided, before anyone watching was aware that he had come back to the land of the living.

It did little good. He could not orient himself. He knew he was sprawled on hard-packed earth, and that the temperature had gone from dry, bitter cold to a heat that stunned and parched and stupefied the mind. He was hungry and thirsty, and no one came to help him. He heard some mechanical and some animal sounds, but they had no meaning and for some time he didn't pay attention to them. He hoped, dimly bitter, that General McFee would be happy that he'd ridden the railroad this far.

"Herr Durell? Sam?"

He heard the thin eerie whisper like a ghost seeking reassurance from the dark, but did not move or allow the tempo of his breathing to change. It was the first tangible sign that he was really among the living.

"Herr Durell? Are you awake?"

When he opened his eyes this time, he saw a faint sliver

65

of white light, long and vertical like an exclamation point, far off to the right. Otherwise, the darkness remained—and the heat. The heat was beyond belief. His lungs strained and gasped, and his body was afire from the desiccating torment. Something sharp and pointed thrust between his shoulders from the hard-packed earth that smelled of dung and urine, both human and animal. He felt very clever then. He opened his eyes a slit and looked to right and left without moving his head. And he promptly felt a cooling, miraculous hand on his forehead.

"Oh, Sam, you are alive, *nein*? You will live!"

Now he could see by the light of that bright and blinding slash in the otherwise total darkness that it was Lisl Steigmann who whispered to him. He could not believe it. He rejected the idea with dismay, and knew he was not yet functioning as he should, still lingering somewhere in that mindless never-never land induced by the drug.

Then he sat upright in the gloom, with alarm clanging and banging along every ragged nerve of his body.

"Lisl?"

"Hush!"

"Where are you?"

"Here. Beside you."

"I can't see you." He felt panic. "My eyes—"

"It's all right. There is no light."

"What is this place?"

"A house—a hut. I do not know where. Please, keep very quiet. They are busy outside."

"Busy?"

"Listen, please. Oh, thank God you are alive! I watched you and thought you would stop breathing any moment and that I'd be left alone in this awful place with your body. . . ."

He could see her now, and came totally awake. She tried to push him back when he sat up, but he put her hands aside and forced himself to his feet. The effort was exhausting in the dizzying heat, and he collapsed again. She did not say anything this time. Her face was a pale, luminous oval drifting nearer and then farther away; her gray eyes were enormous and rounded with astonishment as he tried to pull himself together. She wore the ragged remnants of a woolen black suit she had last been wearing in Munich, but the heat was too much for it and she had discarded the small jacket and hiked up the ragged skirt to expose her long, strong legs for whatever coolness might be obtained. She wore a prim white cotton bra that was hard put to contain her swelling, provocative breasts. Her soft shoulders were slim, somehow vulnerable. Her long, pale hair, almost like a white halo in this unearthly dimness that as yet had no relationship to reality, seemed to drift around the concerned contours of her young face.

"Water?" he whispered.

She nodded hastily, eager to please. "I saved some for you. Do not spit it out, even if it tastes awful. It is all we have."

He understood her warning when she lifted a crude bowl to lips. The water was brackish, almost as salty as the sea, and certainly as warm as the air, which was well over one hundred degrees. He drank the foul stuff carefully, and would have drained it all had not her words suddenly registered.

"How much water do we have?"

"That is all."

"How long have we been here?"

"Two days, I think."

"Two days? And how often have we been given water?"

"Once a day. Forgive me, I know how it seems to you, but—" She made small, instinctual gestures to tidy herself, irrepressibly feminine. She reached for her discarded jacket and Durell checked her, saying: "Don't bother. You'll suffer heat exhaustion if you put that on."

"You were unconscious for so long, I thought they'd given you too much of the drug and that you'd never wake up."

"It wasn't exactly a scientific dosage," he admitted. His head was splitting, with a score of tribal drums beating an ungodly rhythm against his skull. "I think I'm all right now."

He lay back, panting for air in the windowless cell. The room was not large, not more than eight feet square, with its hard dirt floor that clenched in its solidity the stench of urine and dung. The single slit of light came from a wooden door that felt, to his exploring touch, a thousand years old and as tough as steel. The hinges were on the outside. He knelt and hunted with his fingers for a keyhole, and found one, bound in a greasy brass plate; but when he put his eye to it, he could not understand what he saw: a slash of blue, a splash of green, some gray images that refused to focus. He thought he heard a camel braying, and then he was sure he heard a car engine, perhaps a jeep, start up.

67

The voices he heard, however, reassured him. They were Arabic, but too far away to interpret.

He continued his circuit of the cell while Lisl crouched with legs tucked under her and watched, her face turning in the dimness to follow his stubborn moves. There was no crack or crevice in the walls. They were sun-baked clay, with vague designs stenciled on them. He couldn't scratch a hole in them when he dug with his fingernails. He had nothing else to use at hand. His gun, keys, money, pen—everything was cleaned out. The room had a high, beamed ceiling he could not reach. Pausing, he shrugged off his coat and then his shirt. He felt as if he were drowning in the heat. With no windows and no opening in the solid plank door, the room was like an oven collecting the sun's venom.

"How many times do they feed the animals in this zoo, Lisl?" he asked.

"Once each day. Two days, in all. When it was cool, so I think it was early morning. Are you hungry?"

He ignored her question. "What kind of food was it?"

She shook her head. "Lumps of lamb, I think."

"Any left?"

"No, it is taken away."

"Who has that job?"

She seemed reluctant to speak of it. "He's an Arab, I think. He's a little crazy. He smells and he always giggles and he tries to—to make love to me."

From the sounds outside and the crude stencils on the wall, he was sure they were prisoners in some desert oasis. But where? He couldn't guess. And speculation was useless. He leaned back to conserve his strength in the dark heat. Every breath was an effort that brought a searing pain in his chest. But after a time his headache eased. He sipped more of the rancid water, but decided to save as much as he could.

"How did they get you here, Lisl?" he asked.

"I am not sure what happened, to be truthful. I'm afraid I was stupid. When Carole left your hotel room—"

"Why did she go? I told her to stay."

"She changed her mind and decided to speak freely to you. She said she'd hidden some material you would want in the bed, while we attended to her bullet wound—"

"Yes. Have they told you about Carole?"

"No. I know nothing."

He said bluntly: "They murdered her. Not very nicely,

68

either. Just as they kidnapped you, because you didn't obey my instructions, and let someone into the room."

"Carole? She's *dead*?"

"Yes."

"But I thought—when someone knocked, and spoke to me, it was a woman, and I thought she was returning, so I opened the door—"

Durell remembered Mademoiselle Zuzu at the *Oktoberfest* pavilion. It seemed long ago, lost in the past that lacked reality against the starkness of their prison here. Of course, he could not complain. He had asked and hoped for the trip. But he did not like the added complication of Lisl's presence. She was too vulnerable, too lovely and young, and had no real part in the struggle that engaged him. He'd have been happier without her, and yet he was grateful for her company in this place. Then he heard her weeping.

"Take it easy."

"But Carole was my friend."

"She was a Shinbet Agent—Israeli Intelligence Service," he said harshly. "It's a rough business. She knew the risks and the price she might have to pay."

"How can you be so calm, so cruel, like a machine—"

"That's how to survive," he said.

She was silent, plucking at the ragged hem of her skirt hiked above her knees. When she spoke again, her voice was controlled as she told how she had opened the hotel-room door in Munich, expecting Carole, only to feel a blinding pain in her breast and fall unconscious.

"I woke up here. I don't know what happened. I was lying beside you, and I thought you were dead; you didn't seem to be breathing. I tried to get out. I guess I was hysterical and screaming, and that guard came and began to—began to—" She paused and swallowed noisily, like a child fighting hiccups. "Someone else came and stopped him just in time. So he satisfied himself by kicking you a few times."

Well, Durell thought angrily, that explained his bruised ribs that stabbed him every time he took a breath. He began to look forward to seeing this guard Lisl described. He was silent, and Lisl cried softly again, and he was satisfied with that, since it served to release her tensions. Alone here, with only his unconscious body for company, constantly fearing the unnatural attentions of the Arab guard, it was a miracle she hadn't cracked and succumbed to total hysteria.

After a time, she said quietly: "I am sorry, but it is not

69

easy to accept this sort of thing. Carole was my friend, and I cannot put her aside as readily as you do. Everything has happened so quickly and changed so much, since she first came to me and told me about my father . . ."

"Have you seen him?" Durell asked.

"My father? No."

"Not at all? Not since you woke up here?"

"No."

He did not like that. It meant there was another spur line on the underground railway, and perhaps he was on a side track, and Dr. Steigmann had been expressed right to the end of the line, which he wanted to reach himself. But that could not be helped. He had come part of the way, and he was still alive—somewhat to his surprise. There was nothing to do but await developments.

He knew how to be patient, although it never came easily to him. Time in the hut seemed as meaningless as when he was under the influence of the needle that had wiped out everything while he was transported here. The day was endless, but he could judge its progress by the way the heat slowly increased until his senses made everything unreal, and all that was important was the effort it took to take the next tortured breath. There seemed to be no end to the way the temperature soared, but there was certainly a limit to what he and the girl could endure. He became lost in a hot haze of unreality, drifting through oceans of molten lava, when his only focus was the next breath, the girl's gasps, the occasional image of her face and half-naked body drenched in sweat as the day wore on.

No one came to look at them.

No one fed them.

Once, Lisl tore a strip of cloth from her skirt and moistened it in their precious clay water bowl and bathed his forehead with it. He made her squeeze out the smelly stuff and replace it in the drinking bowl, after wetting her lips with it and taking a few drops in his own mouth. She had lost her modesty now, in her desperate effort simply to stay alive. But when his hand brushed her hip accidentally, she remembered, and shrank away.

The dim light in the door faded, the temperature began to drop, and he revived a little. He pushed himself up and went to the wooden panels and tried to look out through the crack. But he still could not define anything out there. He hammered on the door with the heel of his shoe, but no one came.

He was hungry now, with a three-day hunger that grew ravenous as the day's heat slowly evaporated and was replaced by a growing chill. Darkness flowed into the hut. He took off his shoe and twisted the right heel and found the little tool kit in there that the gimmick boys of K Section's lab had given him. The girl watched with careful eyes. A few quick manipulations gave him a tiny lever and screwdriver; but there were no screws in the door, and the chrome-steel pry-bar was too small to be effective. There was a tiny flashlight, but he didn't use it. As a last resort, there was a cyanide pill and a tiny tube of nerve gas. He pocketed the tube, thinking he might use it soon, and replaced the pill. He never liked to touch it. The girl spoke tonelessly.

"We'll never escape, will we?"

"I'm not sure I want to," Durell admitted.

"What does that mean?"

"If we're to find your father, the best chance we have is that they'll take us to him."

"I think I'll never see Papa again. Even so, how could I face him, after doing all this to him?"

"It wasn't your fault."

"Oh, yes. I betrayed him. He came looking for me out of love, I see that now; but I called him terrible things and handed him over to these people. I forced him to it. Where else could he go? I don't blame him if he cooperates with them now."

"Do you think he will?"

"Cooperate?" The word was something filthy, the way she said it. She spoke bitterly. "I drove him to it. What else can he do?" She hugged herself and shivered. In the dim hut, the chill gathered like a pool of icy water on the hard floor. They had no blankets to protect themselves against the coming night. "I think," she said slowly, "Papa is innocent now, mainly because *you* do. Isn't that strange?"

"I'd like to prove enough to acquit him, Lisl," Durell admitted. "But I wouldn't want to hang by the thumbs until that happened."

She seemed not to hear him. "Carole and Major Asche used me, and people lied to me and made me do things I never should have done. Perhaps I'm too naïve to get along in your world, with people like you. It's a very ugly world you and your people have made."

71

"We didn't make the world the way it is. Neither must I accept it, any more than you. Facing reality is always difficult, Lisl. My job is just to keep things on a reasonably sane level. That's all I know how to do."

"Oh, yes, you know the tools of your trade. I'm a tool for you, and so is Papa, and you don't hesitate to break us if it serves your purpose, isn't that right?"

"Sometimes."

It was markedly colder in the hut, now that the sun was down. The girl shivered again. He gave her his coat. He was sure now they were in some desert oasis, to judge by the occasional grunt of a nearby camel. He smelled the smoke of a cooking fire nearby. From far off he heard the guttural murmur of Arabic, but he could not tell how many men were there. The cell grew dark, and he couldn't even see Lisl beside him.

There was nothing to do but wait.

It didn't take long.

Chapter Fourteen

HE HAD DOZED, with his back braced against a corner of the hut, while the girl kept carefully to her side. He didn't know if it was modesty or resentment that made her keep her distance, and he went to sleep wondering where his responsibility for her began and ended. There was no privacy in their cramped cell, and it probably amused their primitive captors to do this to them, he thought vaguely. He heard her teeth chattering in the cold, when only two hours ago they had gasped in the heat. But there was nothing more he could do for her.

He awoke to the sound of a soft, sucking giggle from the open doorway.

The only move he made was to slowly open his eyes. The girl slept, her body dimly curled into a ball, in the starlight that seeped through the opening in the hut. The man's bulk seemed to fill all of the low rectangle of the doorway, looming dark and heavy and infinitely dangerous. A smell of sweat and feces came into the hut with him.

Through slitted eyes, Durell watched him swing his head

toward the sleeping girl. It was the guard. There was a note of drugged indecency in the sound of his laughter. He wore a dirty rag of a burnous and an equally dirty white robe; he carried no visible weapon.

Again there came the animal giggle, a wet sound from the black, open hole of his mouth. Durell did not move. The creature lurched toward the sleeping Lisl, and reached—

The girl awoke with a scream of terror.

Her reaction was swift and instinctive, and her foot lashed out against the shadow that loomed over her. She caught the man's wrist as he groped over her body, and screamed again. But her resistance had no effect. The man threw himself on her with a grunt, panting, as she tried to writhe away.

"Sam! Sam!"

Durell got smoothly to his feet and rapped out a command in Arabic. "Get away, dog. And be careful."

The man had thought he was still unconscious. But whatever his surprise, he reacted as swiftly as a rattlesnake. Durell might have played for freedom at this moment, using the girl, but this wasn't his aim. And he could not abandon her, in any case. The guard, in a swift flowing motion, had yanked Lisl to her feet and used her as a shield before him, and almost with the same gesture, he put a glittering knife to her throat and held it there.

Durell froze.

The man giggled again. "So the effendi is awake, as Allah desired."

"Let her go."

"And if I do not?"

"Your masters will kill you, if I do not."

The man spat at him. "It is you whom Allah has marked for death, not I. As for the houri—"

"You live in a dream. The girl is desirable, true, but you are not yet in Paradise, dog. And never will be, if you disobey the Prophet's command and break your vows as a Dancer for Allah."

"Eh?" The Arab was confused. "And what do you know of such things?"

"Enough. Let her go," he said again.

Lisl's face was white as she faced him with the guard's knife at her throat. "Be careful," she gasped. "He is not sane."

Durell replied harshly in English. "He's sane enough to guess what I'm talking about."

73

It was an impasse. He could not be sure the guard understood him. The man dragged Lisl to the door and then, giggling suddenly, shoved her with a swift forward thrust that made her stumble against Durell. Before he could disentangle himself from her, the heavy door slammed shut, a bolt grated, and all that could be heard was the guard's shrill curses in Arabic, promising all the tortures of the damned to Durell.

Durell held the shuddering girl tightly; he was bathed in a cold sweat. Lisl clung to him as if she would never let go, and gasped: "Thank you. That was the worst yet. He will find some way to kill you, now—some way in which he will not be blamed for your death."

"Don't worry about that."

"Hold me," she whispered. "I'm so cold."

Her teeth chattered, and she was wracked by her convulsive shivering. He eased her to the floor in his corner of the hut and held her close to give her body warmth. Her soft, thick hair was a pale aura against his cheek. Her tears slid with warm saltiness against his mouth. He kissed her gently.

"Is he the only guard you've seen?"

"Y-yes."

"Where have the others gone?"

"I heard someone t-talking English—yesterday, perhaps. I'm not sure when. There is some difficulty in transport, he said. A delay. He—he didn't say how long."

"I heard a jeep earlier."

"It is gone. There is only the camel now." She paused. "He will kill you somehow, Sam. I know it. He just w-wants me. . . ."

"Everything will be all right," he said softly.

But now he did not think so.

Lisl slept in his arms, curled tightly against him. He thought wryly of other times and other women with whom he had spent the night, but he had never imagined a night like this, or a woman like Lisl. She moved him by her confusion and her need to orient herself in a world that had suddenly turned a brutal, unexpected face to her. He did not know how to comfort her; he couldn't even reassure her about her father. Obviously, Dr. Steigmann had been spirited out of Munich by another route on the underground. Where Steigmann might be was anyone's guess. The surrounding desert was hostile and enormous in its emptiness.

He might be anywhere within an area covering hundreds of bleak miles. Even if Durell wanted to escape now, he might find he had exchanged the relative safety of this miserable hut for a painful death from thirst, heat and cold.

He could have done without the complication of Lisl's presence, but as he held her sleeping body close to him, he felt a need to protect and help her. It was not her fault that she had been tricked into this affair. Part of the responsibility was his. True, in his business, you could not worry about the next man. You carried on, and if your friend was in trouble, you could not save him at the risk of blowing the assignment. He could not begin to explain this to the girl. Nor could he explain to himself why he felt this urgent need to respond to her. He only knew he could not leave her unguarded to the future.

He dozed and awoke and slept again. The hut was cold. Now and then, the girl in his arms whimpered as nightmares touched her. At dawn she awoke with a small scream and leaped away from him, wriggling across the floor to her own corner.

"I'm sorry—I didn't mean—"

"Everything was quiet, Lisl. Don't be afraid."

He saw her dimly in the dawn light that seeped through the crack in the door. She made ineffectual attempts to straighten her pale hair. Her days in the hut had taken their toll of her clothing, and she was no longer the proud, straight-shouldered girl of Munich.

"I'm sorry to be so much trouble. If only I knew *why* I was here!" she protested.

"Well, they know your father loves you, and if he doesn't cooperate with them, they'll use you to make him do so." She looked as if she didn't understand, and he added: "They'll threaten to harm you, to make your father do as they wish."

"But why should he do anything for me now?" Her voice was a mournful query. "Why should he care about me, after what I did to him?"

"Lisl, the fact that they took you is the best hope you have that your father is really innocent. It means he didn't plan this and didn't come with the Dancers willingly, don't you see? Otherwise, they wouldn't need you."

She was thoughtful. "But then, why are we here in this place, instead of being with him?"

75

"I don't know. You heard them say something about a snag in their transport system?"

"Yes, but—"

"Then we'll just have to be patient."

It was easier to suggest than to practice. An hour after dawn, the Dancer guard opened the door carefully and shoved in two evil-smelling bowls of fatty lamb and a third bowl of stagnant water. Durell tried to glimpse the outside area beyond him, but the light was blinding after the darkness of the hut, and he could only make out a cluster of date palms, a tangled mass of oranges and figs behind mud walls, a few square, yellow houses and a fence of barbed wire. A high, dazzling ridge of sand loomed beyond the village. The sand was helpful. The deserts of the Middle East varied from flinty rock to semi-grassed areas, aside from the oceans of drifting sand. It gave him a better idea of their locale.

"What is your name, dog?" he asked the guard.

"My name is known to Allah, blessed be His name."

"And is Mohammed his prophet?"

"All men know this." The Arab giggled. "And all men know a Second Prophet has been named by the Blessed One."

"I would like to meet and talk with your Prophet."

"Such a blessing may be granted to you." Again the giggle rasped like a fingernail drawn across slate. "You may not welcome the vision, effendi. It may blind you. Or leave you less than a man, eh?"

The guard suddenly made an unmistakable sweep with his knife that threatened Durell with mutilation. Durell stepped back, and the Arab grinned.

"This makes all men afraid. And how is the houri today?" He turned his head to regard Lisl. "She is very beautiful, and could be amusing, I think."

"On your life," said Durell.

"Who knows what will be done with you, effendi? I have a feeling we are all forgotten."

"Then your friends have gone?"

The man grinned. "Ah, no. There are thousands with me, all about us!"

He whirled suddenly, spinning on his dirty, naked toes, and flashed his knife in glittering arcs while a strange ululating song came from his throat. He leaped forward at Lisl, seized her, and held her in an obscene embrace for just the instant it took Durell to start for him. The Arab

76

released her and threw her to the dirt floor and jumped to the doorway with a scream of defiance, laughing as he bolted it again from the outside. His guttural screams came for another moment, then ended.

Durell knelt beside the cowering girl.

"Are you hurt?"

"N-no. But he is quite mad, isn't he?"

"It's the hashish. You can smell it on him."

She said desperately: "Can't we get away? I'd rather die at once, than stay like this. Don't you *want* to escape? You could have tried just now—"

"And should we abandon your father? They'll take us to him, eventually."

"Oh. I see. You're willing to risk it?"

"That's what I'm here for." He took the bowls of food and said, "It's time to eat. Whether you want to or not, you must. We may be here for some time, and I'm hungry enough to eat worse stuff than this."

She shook her head. "I couldn't. I'm all upset inside. Here we're in this awful place, with no decency, no privacy, like two animals in a cage—"

"The animals are out there, Lisl. Eat."

The heat built up rapidly as the sun rose in the sky. In an hour, it was all they could do in their airless little room to keep breathing. Durell made the girl lie flat on her back, and warned her not to exert herself too much. The following hours were a nightmare, as yesterday had been. He had to concentrate on simply staying alive, and their chances did not look good now.

He thought that something had gone wrong with the Dancers' organization. It was possible they were to be abandoned in this lost and hellish place. The same thought came to Lisl after a time. She got up and crawled to the thick paneled door and pressed her ear to it. She listened for a long time, then turned her pale face toward Durell.

"No one is out there. I don't hear a sound." Her voice lifted. "Have they just left us here to die?"

It occurred to Durell that the Dancer guard would hardly go off without Lisl, who fascinated him. But he did not add to her burdens by pointing this out to her. Just the same, he felt a twinge of anxiety and joined her at the door. It was true. There was only silence.

"He must be sleeping," he suggested.

"Can we get out, then?"

"I don't know if we should. It's a gamble, Lisl. If we try to escape and fail, he'll have an excuse to kill us. And if we succeed, we may never find your father again."

She said dully: "We won't find him, anyway, like this. It's hopeless. I know what's going to happen to me."

He began to think she was right, and for some moments considered abandoning his plan by making an effort to escape. Simply as an exercise, to keep his mind from the stupefying heat, he prowled the hut to look for a way out. He spent an hour going over every inch of the stenciled walls, and another half-hour using his belt buckle and his shoe, which were all he had that could be used as tools, to dig through the hard-packed floor. He might as well have scraped at iron. After long minutes of sweaty, exhausting effort, he had gained less than half an inch at the base of the back wall. Lisl offered to spell him, her interest aroused, but he told her to save her strength. It was useless. There was no way out. As for the door, it was too solid, and he could find no inner hinges or means of getting through the thick planking.

And everything was silent outside.

Through the night, he felt the ordeal steadily sap his will and strength. Another day or two, and he would no longer offer any obstacle to the Dancer, if he were still out there, when he tried to take Lisl.

Lisl slept in his arms again, her mood changed.

"We're going to die here," she whispered. "How can you be so calm about it? Are you really so brave?"

"I'm just as afraid as you are, Lisl."

"No, you have courage. And even if you are cruel, too, you can be gentle. You helped clean me of my hatred, do you know? I hated Papa and never listened to anything good about him, even when in my childhood I believed him dead and good riddance. But you showed me the other side of the coin. You are willing to admit he might be innocent. You are willing to hope and believe. You made me ashamed, and at first I turned my hatred against myself. But that is wrong, too. We are all just victims of these events."

"You're growing up, Lisl."

"If you've been thinking of me as a child, I am not. I am a woman."

He smiled as he held her. "I'm aware of that."

"Then don't treat me as a child. I know we are going to

78

die here. Something went wrong with their plans and we are abandoned here, and they don't care what happens to us. We can't escape. We'll die of the heat and thirst here. Isn't that what you think, too?"

"I don't know."

"And if we are going to die—" She paused. She turned in his arms, trembling, but not with the cold now. "Sam, we have so little time left. . . ."

He kissed her, meaning to be gentle with her, but her arms came around his neck and she responded with a wild passion that was startling at first, and then it evoked an inevitable response. The hut was cold and dark. Silence enveloped them.

"Sam . . ."

She kissed him and moved beside him in the darkness and he felt the sudden silken shock of her bare thighs against him and the soft and urgent pressure she exerted. They were alone in an empty sea, a desert that lifted and fell in frozen waves, waiting with sullen hostility to destroy them.

Chapter Fifteen

NO ONE came to the hut in the morning. They had no food and no water. Silence waited beyond the dark ugliness of their primitive prison, an echoing vastness beyond the imagination. When the sun came up, the heat struck with toxic, incredible strength, dulling their senses until they each had only a desperate urge to survive. Hunger and thirst turned them into torpid entities, waiting only for the end.

It seemed that Lisl was right. They were deserted.

Toward noon, he made up his mind that the worst had happened, that something had really gone wrong with the Dancers' plans. He and Lisl were forgotten and ignored. He had no choice now. It was no longer a matter of remaining a willing prisoner in order to follow the trail to its end. The end had another meaning now. If they were to survive, he had to escape.

He spent the long hours digging with bloody fingers and hands, using the belt buckle and his shoe, at the hard dirt floor. It was as adamant as the walls of the hut. He knew he was draining precious strength with the effort, but there was no help for it. When he had to stop and rest, Lisl took up the labor.

By nightfall he had dug only a shallow depression eight inches deep. The base of the hut wall was still sunk somewhere below his reach.

The little oasis was silent outside. An occasional whimper of a vagrant wind made the sand hiss against the doorway. On that next night, Lisl lay quietly in his arms. He was alarmed about her. He could not guess at the limits of her endurance, but considering her recent trials, he did not hope that she could last much longer. His own thirst was very severe now. Hunger cramped him, and the cold of the desert night had a new intensity. Lisl spoke very little, and her mind turned back to dim memories of her childhood. She tried to recall anything she could about her father, but Dr. Hubertus Steigmann had fled with the Nazi collapse, when she was still in her infancy, and she could remember nothing. She had spent her life in compensating for the evils done by her country, and she still felt a sense of national guilt, but Durell had ignited a spark of hope for her father's personal innocence. She talked of this gratefully, and then she slept, her breathing light and shallow, and he held her quietly and let the long night hours drift endlessly by.

On the morning of the third day, he was desperate. The thick silence continued outside the hut, echoing with strange ringing noises he heard within his mind. He knew the toll of thirst and hunger was taking effect. When he looked at Lisl, he did not think she would live to the next dawn.

He continued to dig at the base of the back wall. No one came with food or water. He made the girl sit quietly when she offered to help. The heat was too much for her, and he worked alone.

Toward noon, when he had to stop, gasping, stripped to the waist and slippery with sweat, he heard more ringing noises and the sounds of a drum and the high ululation of someone's song. The singing was repetitive, starting on a thin high note and drifting down and down, then pausing to begin again its atonal notes at the top. He thought it was all in his mind, a fevered impression so real it made him believe someone was dancing and singing out there. . . .

Lisl gave no sign that she had heard the sounds. In the dark oven of the hut, she lay with her eyes closed, her breath lifting and falling in a shallow rhythm.

80

The tambour was distinct, the thin ululation clear and somehow menacing. He covered his ears and heard only the thud of blood that surged heavily in his temples. When he took his hands away, the singing came clearer.

It was no delusion. Someone was out there. Someone had come back to the oasis.

Or perhaps had never gone away.

Perhaps the Dancer had simply enjoyed an exercise in subtle Arabic cruelty, displaying patience of an exquisite type in letting the last two days go by without visiting them.

"Lisl," Durell whispered.

She opened her eyes.

"Lisl, he's still out there."

"The guard?"

"Can't you hear him?"

She sat up, her face taut with strain. At last she nodded. "I thought it was in my dream."

"He's out there, all right." Durell wet his parched lips. His mouth felt full of cotton. "He's coming this way. He's waited it out, Lisl, you understand? To weaken me, and make sure that we've been abandoned by his bosses. Now he's dancing out there in the sun, and coming for us. We'll have only one chance."

"What can we do?"

"Kill him," said Durell.

"Can you do it?"

"I've got to do it."

"But if you fail—"

He looked at her, and she understood, and she gathered herself together to stand up. She wavered on her feet and leaned heavily against him. "What do you want me to do?"

"Encourage him, Lisl. Occupy his attention."

"How far?"

"As far as necessary."

She looked away and made a curious gesture to tidy her thick, pale hair. Her skirt was badly torn and her long, tanned thigh showed through the rents. She wore only her bra and skirt in the black heat that filled their little prison.

"I'm not very enticing," she said ruefully.

"Call him," said Durell. "He might dance for hours out there, otherwise. And we won't last that long. Call him now."

"All right, Sam."

His weapons were several, after all. He had his shoe, his belt, and the tiny tube of nerve gas he had taken from the

81

hollow heel of his shoe when he first awoke in this place. He decided against the gas. In this confined cell there was every chance that he and Lisl would also fall victim to the stuff, which worked instantaneously. It had to be the belt, then. It could be as lethal a weapon as any.

Lisl stood at the door. At his nod, she cried out loudly, putting a plea and a promise in her words that could not be misunderstood. At a signal, she paused, and Durell listened. The thud of the drum and the shrill singing went on without pause; he could hear the stamp of feet in the dust as the Dancer sang his song of praise to the Second Prophet of Allah. There was a mad ecstasy in the singing that worried Durell. Perhaps nothing could penetrate the man's frenzy.

Lisl called out again and beat feebly against the hut door. Durell made her wait. The music and song went on, but the beat of naked feet in the dust outside was just beyond the panel now, and when he pressed his ear to the door, he heard the heavy breathing of the Dancer as he whirled in the harsh sunlight beyond their prison.

"Once more," he whispered to Lisl.

She nodded and called again, "Please, can't you understand? I need food, water—I'll do anything. . . ."

It was questionable whether the Dancer understood English. But there was no mistake about Lisl's meaning.

The drum stopped abruptly.

The man's breathing was like that of an animal in heat, just beyond the thick panel, quick and hot and harsh.

There was a shrill scream of triumph that shattered the hot silence like a lance hurled through glass. Durell flattened against the wall beside the door, winding his leather belt into a garrote between his hands. Lisl retreated slowly to a corner. She looked young and helpless, without defense. But her eyes trusted him and pleaded with him not to fail her. When the heavy iron lock suddenly rattled, he nodded.

For some moments, the door did not open. Silence flowed back. Not even the Dancer's panting breath could be heard.

Then, with a flash of speed, the Dancer burst open the door and in the glare of sunlight that temporarily blinded them, he leaped in, legs bent, the knife flashing in a wild, deadly arc around him. He landed with a thud in the center of the hut, beyond Durell's reach as he stood against the wall. A shrill yelp of triumph came from the man's twisted mouth and he made a gurgling sound and thrust and jabbed the knife menacingly at Durell and shouted something that could not be understood except by the devils to whom the man prayed.

"Effendi, do you hunger? And do you thirst, little one? Ahmed brings you life and joy! Ahmed brings you the peace of death!"

There was no chance of taking him by surprise now. His wild leap, which would have done justice to a ballet master, had carried him in a single flashing movement beyond reach to the other end of the hut. Lisl had no chance to escape. The man giggled and reached out for her with a claw and caressed her shoulder. But his eyes flashed like white crescents as he watched Durell.

"Did you miss me, *habibi*?" he crooned. "Did you long to hear my steps, bringing you drink and food? I have much food, my white dove. Much wine, although Allah forbids it, and sweet, cool water from the well, so cool it makes the drops bead on the pitcher, delicious as it slides down one's throat. . . ."

"Please, please," Lisl moaned.

"I cannot understand your words, habibi," the Dancer grinned. "But you are a true pearl of Paradise for one who follows the Second Prophet, even as he promised us when we made our vows to follow him."

"Do you speak of Selim El-Raschid?" Durell asked, to distract him.

"I speak of Allah's anointed one, the true messenger who will spread fire and sword throughout the world, if the world fails to accept him." The Dancer paused and giggled again, then suddenly reached out to pinch at Lisl's rigid body. Lisl obeyed Durell's instructions. She did not move. She even managed a weak, uncertain smile at the evil-smelling man with the flashing knife.

Durell was accustomed to the glare of the sunlight now. The day was later than he had thought. The Dancer had left the door open, as if to entice him, and he saw again the empty squalor of the hamlet gathered around the oasis, the dusty palms and tamarisks, the sand-colored huts and mud walls baking in the hot sun under the brazen sky. There was no car, no camel in sight. The empty dunes beyond were like giant waves frozen in waiting, waiting to crash and fall and bury the tiny, ghostly settlement.

"Sam . . ." Lisl breathed tightly.

"Let him do what he wants."

"I don't know if I can endure it."

"It won't be long. Keep him busy."

"I—I'll see if I can."

The Dancer paid no attention to their words. He put his knife between his teeth and pulled Lisl toward him; his odor, like that of a tomcat, filled the hut. But those flashing crescent eyes never left Durell, who knew now the speed and precision with which this man could move, faster than any enemy he had encountered before. The Dancer, with a swift clawing movement, hooked a finger in Lisl's bra, tore it free, and flung it aside. Lisl moaned softly. Her arms were rigid at her sides. Durell knew he could wait no longer.

"Dog, there is no pleasure in a frightened woman," he said quietly.

"There is pleasure even in a dead one," the Dancer said. His teeth shone as they gripped his knife. His words hissed around the steel. "You will stay there, and not interfere. Your turn will come later."

"You're not afraid to do this, without your friends to help you?" Durell taunted.

"They are all gone, effendi. And tonight I must go, too."

"Are we forgotten, then?"

"By Allah and by Shaitan, too, but not by Ahmed, the Dancer-for-God." The man grinned. "So you are both for my pleasure and your pain. Why does the girl moan so much?"

"She needs water. She is very weak."

"Why does she shiver, when it is so hot in here?"

"She fears you. She is hungry and thirsty."

"And you do not fear me? My knife thirsts for certain portions of your flesh."

"We shall see."

Durell started toward him. He could not wait. His thirst was a fever that blotted out all caution. Nor could he delay, because of Lisl. Her rigidity was catatonic, and the least offense she might give the Dancer could result in a single, instantaneous slash at her throat, too fast for him to check. He made no attempt to surprise the Dancer, and he did not hide the belt in his hand. Ahmed's eyes flickered to it, and his teeth gleamed around the knife. He pushed Lisl's half-naked form to one side and grunted softly and began to sing, a thin, whining melody that had no rhythm or meaning. He took the knife from his mouth and held it with its point toward Durell and began to circle the hut,

84

moving in closer to where Durell now waited in the center of the floor.

"American, you are too soft-hearted to watch what I do to the little habibi? Then she must watch what I do to you, eh? You will give me warm pleasure when I adorn you with your blood and rearrange your members."

"You talk too much," Durell said. "You talk more than you can perform."

"Eeh-aye! You shall choke on your own words, and on your own flesh that I shall make you eat, effendi."

"Come ahead," Durell said.

Lisl made a small sound, but he did not look at her. Everything would be over in the next few seconds. The knife made shining arabesques that flashed through the dim air before his eyes. The Dancer leaped, screamed, and feinted. Durell was not drawn into a premature attack. His hands sweated on the leather belt gripped in his fists. It was a poor defense against that weaving blade. One proper slash of the Dancer's knife would slice through it as if it were paper. The tiny room was thick with the Arab's odor again. His breath came in quick, impatient grunts. . . .

Durell moved first, after all. He had held his two fists before him, the strap pulled tight between them for a garrote attack. But now he released his left hand and flicked the buckle end of the belt out with a sudden whipcrack of a blow that made the metal fastener snap between the Dancer's eyes, on the bridge of his nose. The septum was crushed in and one eye turned into a bloody red egg that slid down the man's cheek from the ruined socket. Ahmed screamed and clapped a hand to his face and shrieked again and struck with the knife. There was no escape in these close quarters. The point hissed through cloth and ran like a red-hot wire slicing through Durell's left arm. The Dancer staggered, but was never quite off balance. Durell jumped, caught the buckle in his left hand again, and whipped the leather over the Dancer's shaved head and yanked it tight about the straining throat. The Dancer jerked and writhed and his knife whirled in a wild arc above his head and came slashing down like the strike of a snake. Durell pulled them both off balance to the hard floor. They rolled over and over, toward Lisl who crouched, big-eyed, in her corner. The Arab was a powerful man. Even with his ghastly wound, his eye out of its socket, he fought like a wild animal, his body slippery and writhing with

85

muscles. Durell could not hold him for more than a few seconds. Thirst and hunger had taken its toll.

"Lisl . . . !"

She was too far gone to be of much help. But she came at the Dancer with long, clawing fingernails and raked his arm and clung to his knife wrist until the blood came. The sting distracted him. He lurched and rolled over and over in the dust toward the doorway, and Durell followed, his belt still choking off the man's breath. But how long could he hold on? He did not know. His strength ebbed quickly.

Lisl crawled after them, more animal than human. The man's arm and hand holding the knife was momentarily flat, extended across the floor. She fell on it, her naked body gleaming in the harsh sunlight that poured blindingly upon them. Her face was savage. They were no longer human, in that tiny place. The smell of blood and filth and death filled the air.

The Dancer kicked spasmodically. His hand came up, trying to loosen the belt, then gave up and scratched at Durell's head. Durell jerked out of reach of those powerful fingers. Lisl gasped as the knife point pricked her. The sounds she made were not intelligible.

Then the Dancer suddenly went limp.

Durell did not relax his grip. He did not trust him. Ahmed's face was horrible to look at. Then all at once Lisl screamed, a sound of utter fury, and Durell saw that she had the Arab's knife. She plunged it hard into the man's writhing belly, pulled it free, and drove it in again. The body jerked and kicked.

"Stop it, Lisl. . . ."

She struck the Dancer again.

"He's dead, Lisl. . . ." Durell said.

He did not know which of them had actually killed the man. He released the belt carefully and the body rolled to one side, awkwardly. Lisl's eyes were blind. He wrenched the blade from her and threw it away and got to his knees, swaying. He tried to stand up, and could not. He looked at the open doorway. They were free.

Chapter Sixteen

LISL WAS sick. She crouched on hands and knees in the shade of a mud wall and a dusty date palm and threw up, or tried to, for there was nothing in her stomach. Her thick hair was tangled, falling in a screen about her naked shoulders, and she looked small and wretched and oblivious to the empty oasis around them. Durell got to his feet and went to the stone-coped well nearby. It took all his strength to draw the bucket, made of a gasoline can, up to the surface. He tasted the water and found it sweet and pure, unlike the brackish stuff the guard had been giving them. It was just another small evidence of the man's brutal spite.

He drank sparingly, although he shook with the craving to gulp it all down with reckless greed. Reviving, he carried the rest to the girl, who did not look up from her kneeling position. He poured the water over her, and at the shock she wrenched sidewise, and then turned a tormented face upward to him.

"Have some of this. But be very careful."

She could not hold the heavy can, so he poured some into his cupped palm and she drank from his hand, and then he gave her another small portion and when she was through she pressed her lips to his palm and sighed.

"What have I done, Sam?"

"Nothing. We're free, and you must put it out of your mind."

"But I killed him. I did it again and again."

"No, I'd already strangled him."

"What does it matter? I was like a savage, I wanted to cut and stab and hack—"

"Stop it, Lisl. It does no good."

She covered her face with her hands. "I didn't know such things about myself. I never dreamed I was like that."

"We all are, when it comes to survival. Can you stand up now?"

"Help me," she said.

He got her to her feet. She leaned heavily on him and he said: "Next order on the agenda is some food."

"Where are we?"

"I don't know yet. We'll explore a bit, and find out."

There were some dozen houses ranged behind walls around the tiny well, many of them with fallen roofs and with sand choking their broken doorways. The small gardens had grown rank and wild, filled with figs and pomegranates. The afternoon shadows were long as they walked from one to the other in search of the Dancer's quarters. They found a blanket roll in the largest house, a pink-walled affair that reeked of hashish smoke. Cactus and thorny shrubs grew around it, mixed with the high stalks of papyrus that shot up around a tiny pool in the back. Beside the blanket were some tins of food and, equally important, a Russian-made automatic rifle and a dozen clips for it, rolled in a silken prayer rug of delicate design. The hot wind blew curtains of sand against the boles of the date palms, making a lonely whisper. Durell opened one of the tins of beef, and they ate it cold and gelatinous, as it was.

"Why is no one here?" Lisl asked. She would not look at him. "It's so deserted—"

"That's the big question. I'd like to find out just where this place is."

"I want to get away," she said suddenly. "The others might come back, and when they find out what we've done—"

"Don't feel guilty. We had no choice."

"But the way we did it, like a couple of beasts—"

"Unfortunately, our world isn't too far removed from the jungle." They sat in the shade of the pink house, since the sun was too strong for them to expose themselves to its crushing heat. "We take pride in our civilization," he said quietly, "but the stupidity and greed you read about in any daily newspaper is proof enough of the fantasy we've created. We take in the so-called emergent nations and give them seats in the U.N., and when they hold hostages and threaten cannibalism, and we attempt to rescue the poor souls, the other side screams 'imperialism' with incredible hypocrisy and disregard for human civilization. The big lie and the brazen insult are the first things these new countries learn to manipulate—like a child learning dirty words. And if you and I had to resort to killing just now, it was in order to survive."

"Even if we go down to their savage level?"

"I never adhered to Gandhi's passivity," Durell said. "To survive is a basic instinct. The Dancer was going to kill us

—or me, anyway. He had worse plans for you. Slavery isn't unknown in this part of the world."

She shuddered. "I'm sorry. I must seem foolish and emotional to you."

"We're both exhausted. Come along. There must be a reasonably clean pool somewhere. We could use a bath."

"Shouldn't we run away at once? I mean, suppose someone comes back for us?"

"I don't think that will happen."

He had already looked about for transportation—for the camel he had hoped to find tethered somewhere, or a jeep. There was nothing. The oasis was ghostly in its isolation.

They found a pool in one of the back gardens, shaded by a mud wall and tall traveler palms. Flies buzzed in black swarms under the trees. He carried the auto-rifle with him and helped the girl over the wall.

"In you go. You'll find it refreshing."

There was a green scum on the water which the girl viewed with distaste. "Clothes and all?"

"What's left of it needs washing. Take your time—we can't start until sundown, when the heat goes."

After their days in the black hut, the freedom of sky and wind was like a blessing. When the girl slid into the water, he turned to a small minaret nearby and found at its base a ragged wooden sign with Egyptian Army inscriptions on it, indicating this was Post 24, Dir-el-Birba. He was not sure where this might be, and he climbed painfully to the top of the square tower for the view. There was a dim track that meandered out of sight across what seemed an endless waste of sand dunes. It went westward into the sun until it was lost in the frozen combers beyond view. They would have to go that way. To venture into the trackless area in another direction would mean a quick death from sunstroke and thirst.

He hated to admit defeat. His escape was not a victory, but a setback, from which his mission might never gain success. True, if he could reach safety and cable his data on the Dancers to General McFee in Washington, he might set wheels in motion to crush the outward evidence of the human smuggling operation. But only the smallest tentacles of the octopus would be cut off. There was more, much more, to the Dancers than simply an underground railway. There was a wild fanaticism to the movement that could cause one of those world upheavals that left death and devastation in its wake. Somewhere in this vast, empty desert was a center, a heart of evil that had to be struck a quick, sure blow. By escaping, he had lost his chance to be escorted there by his own enemies, however dangerous the way.

"Sam?"

He heard Lisl call thinly and he climbed down the stairway of the minaret and returned to the pond. She had shed her clothes and, having washed them, was swimming in the tiny pool. She looked refreshed, and there was a brighter light in her gray eyes. Her body with its pale provocative curves shone as she turned on her side and then floated on her back.

"Sam, come in here. You must wash that wound."

He had almost forgotten the thin gashes cut in his arm by the Dancer's knife. "In a moment. Stay there."

She was instantly alarmed. "Where are you going?"

"Back to the hut. Not for long. Wait for me."

The Dancer lay with bared, glistening teeth in the doorway of their prison hut. Durell pulled him into the sunlight where he could examine the body more closely. The clothing consisted of a secondhand European jacket and baggy trousers with worn leather slippers, which he had taken off before leaping in to his death. He had been a powerful man, well-muscled, with the brown skin of a desert Arab and curious scars on his cheeks. Durell opened the shirt and saw gray lice crawling there. Under the shirt he found a small golden chain ending in a heavy medallion that could also have been gold.

He broke it free and turned it over in his hands. Immediately his mind leaped back to Munich, and the clue that poor Carole Bainbury had managed to yield to him before her savage death. He recalled her postcard from the museum, the Alte Pinakothek, of a Byzantine mosaic with its curious design of a dancing monk.

The same portrait was etched on the gold medallion worn by the Dancer, with a faded and illegible Greek inscription. Durell stared long at the curious little figure, with its transfiguring halo, the arms uplifted and one leg raised in a graceful and ecstatic dancing posture.

"Sam?"

It was Lisl again. He heard no alarm in her voice. Only

90

a quiet invitation. He pocketed the medallion and walked back through the shadows of the oasis to the mud-walled pool, where she waited for him.

Chapter Seventeen

THE MOON was cold and hostile in the infinite darkness of space, regarding them with mockery as they toiled along the faint trace of a road leading to the west. The path wound among bleak dunes that at times towered over them like giant sea breakers about to shatter themselves over their heads. The Milky Way was a silver ribbon of brilliance across the sky. Durell had found an old burnous in one of the huts and the girl used it to fabricate some kind of protection over her own torn clothing. She had bandaged his arm, after washing it in the well water; it felt stiff, but no muscles were torn, and his fingers flexed well enough around the solid comfort of the automatic rifle he'd taken from the Dancer.

He had done all he could. He had filled the dead man's canteen and packed the remaining tins of food in a small sack that the girl insisted on carrying. They did not speak much as they trudged along. It was as if the empty spaces above and around them, the cold reeling sky, and the frozen sea of sand inhibited the sound of human voices. There was only the gritty echo of their shoes and the occasional slide and hiss of sand as they crossed drifts that filled the dim path.

After a time they rested on a dune. The toll taken by their captivity was greater than he had expected. Lisl would not be able to go on for long. The worst of it was that he had no idea of the distance ahead, or what dangers waited for them beyond the looming sands. His eyes scanned the crests for signs of life, but the only movement came from the thin plumes of sand blown hissing by the cold night wind. The girl moved into his arms, shivering.

"How far must we go, Sam?"

"I don't know yet."

"Do you really believe we'll make it?"

"We must think so."

She was silent. Then she said: "I know you're worried because every step takes us farther from my father, and what you've set out to do."

"It can't be helped. Don't worry about it, Lisl. All we can do is concern ourselves with the moment."

"But there isn't much time left for us."

"I don't intend to die here," he said flatly. "Come on, get to your feet."

"What's the use?"

"Get up," he said, and his voice was harsh.

"But I'm so tired. It's all hopeless, and you know it. You're cruel. Why can't we just stay here?"

"Because we'll die, if we do."

"It's as good a place as any, isn't it?"

"Then why did you help me kill the Dancer?"

His face in the moonlight was adamant. He knew better than Lisl how slim their chances were. He had been in difficult spots before, but never one like this. Without her, he'd have remained at the oasis as long as the Dancer's scant supplies held out, hoping to be picked up again by the Dancer apparatus. Why had he yielded to sentiment? There was no room for such sentiment in his business. Lisl was lovely and helpless, confused in her attitudes toward him and her father. She was of no importance to the assignment that had brought him here. In other times, he'd had to sacrifice good men for the success of a mission, men who knew the risks and accepted defeat as part of the world they worked in. But perhaps that was just the point. This girl, this amateur, did not know the risks, and was simply a victim of a maneuver that had dragged her into this mess in her open-eyed innocence. He could not abandon her.

They walked, rested, and walked again. Lisl's pace was increasingly slow. Finally he had to help her, his arm supporting her sagging body. She began to moan, and she whispered to herself in German. The moon reached its zenith and slid down toward the west. He had no idea of the time. His watch had been taken from him at some point in the past days. Their rest halts grew longer and more frequent.

When the moon had dipped almost to the western horizon, he caught a glimpse of movement that did not belong to the shifting sand or tricky shadows. It was only a glimmer, quickly come and gone, atop a dune behind them. He was not sure he had seen it, and he said nothing to Lisl. His senses might be playing tricks on him. He watched and waited.

When it came again, he was not certain if it was human

or animal, but it was there, and it was real. The third time settled the question. Moonlight glinted on metal and glass. They were being watched through night glasses.

It might be an Egyptian Army patrol, in which case their lives were assured, if not a way out of their difficulties. On the other hand, the Dancers might be on their trail, ironically having arrived at the abandoned oasis shortly after their escape. Their path was easy to follow in the sand. He listened, but he heard no sound of distant engines that might betray a desert jeep.

He said nothing to Lisl, and they walked on. After twenty minutes, they halted again. The desert had not changed. In all the cold hours of the night, they had seen no sign of human habitation, no path or road that might lead them somewhere useful.

In the shadows of the next dune he watched again, keeping himself in apparent repose. After a moment he caught the shadow again, a ghost of substance, and then again the glint of glass reflecting the waning moonlight. They would soon move into the darkest period before dawn. It was now or never, he decided.

"Lisl, I'm going to leave you for a few minutes. Stay here and don't move, and act as if you're asleep."

"That will not be difficult. But what is it?"

"I'm not sure. If I don't come back—"

It was a mistake to alarm her. She started up with a betraying jerk, and he held her down roughly. "Be still. We're being watched."

"Watched? By whom? What—?"

"Keep your voice down. It carries in a place like this. Just do as I say."

"But I don't want you to leave me!"

"It will be all right."

He had chosen the deep shadow of a dune in which to halt, and he did not think the secret observer on the other side of the sand trough, where the road meandered, could see them clearly. He walked off, holding the Russian rifle in his left hand, and followed the long shadow for several hundred yards, until he was sure he could not be seen crossing the path. Then he darted over, crouching low, and climbed through the yielding sand of the opposite dune, open to the moonlight.

He flattened down just below the crest and waited for more long moments. Now he heard a sound other than that

93

of the wind and the whispering sand. A dog barked, far away.

His feet kept sliding in the yielding dune. It seemed a long way back as he progressed. Pausing, he searched the opposite side of the sand valley for Lisl, and it took some time to locate her. Oriented by her position, he circled wide and climbed again, cursing the sand that slid and hissed from under his feet.

Finally he saw the shadow, lying prone on the crest above him, night glasses glued to his face, watchful and dangerous. Only one of them. Good. Everything about the man indicated complete attention on Lisl's dim shadow. Durell shifted the gun to his right hand and climbed up behind him. He took his time. He saw the shine of moonlight like a wet fingertip running along the barrel of the other's rifle. And then he was close enough—

The sand betrayed him at the last moment, but it was too late for the silent watcher. He grunted and twisted about, booted foot upraised as Durell leaped for him. A hard heel caught him in the knee, but the blow was short and not strong enough to affect him. As the man twisted on his back, his face a bearded mask in the pale starlight, Durell landed on him with all his weight, the rifle held horizontally now, and he slammed the barrel down across the thick throat.

The yielding sand kept him from crushing the man's larynx and killing him outright. But it was enough to make him helpless instantly.

"Hold it, hold it," Durell whispered.

A gurgle of pain came from the watcher. He jerked about, trying to get free, and clawed for his rifle in the sand nearby, and then lay still and quiet and utterly motionless as Durell pinned him. A sound like odd laughter came from him.

Durell eased up a bit.

"Sam? Sam Durell?"

He eased up a little more. "Turn your head."

The man turned so his face was exposed to the moonlight. He was smiling ruefully.

It was Major Simon Asche.

Chapter Eighteen

DURELL let him up. After the shock of the brief attack, his nerves were jangled. Asche was still the barrel-chested man of Munich whom he had last seen in stunned grief over Carole Bainbury's murder. But there were subtle differences. He had let his beard grow in the past few days, and his clothes, which were still vaguely European, now had that secondhand shabbiness of those worn by most city Arabs. His eyes had changed the most. This man, with his reputation as an archaeologist and soldier, who perhaps by nature was a mild and gentle person, wishing only for his scholarly pursuits, seemed buried behind the cold and impersonal look in his brown eyes. His mouth smiled, and it meant nothing.

Simon guessed at his reaction.

"What do you see, my friend?" he said quietly.

"I'm not sure. I didn't expect you. Are you alone?"

"Quite alone, here. But we have friends waiting for us in Cairo. It's not far."

"Egypt is dangerous for you," Durell said.

Simon's laugh was a harsh bark. "I'd be shot out of hand as a spy, if they caught me. But they won't. I'll see to that. Anyway, I couldn't leave you here, could I?"

"How did you find us?"

"I had five days—quite enough. Will you let me up, please? We're allies, after all, whether you like it or not."

"I don't object to that. But answer my question."

Asche considered Durell for a moment. "When they took you at the Cairo Dancers' pavilion in Munich, it was easy to trace you. I admit I was slow—I was stunned and not quite professional in my attitude about Carole's death. But I put some pressure on our mutual collaborator, the little Inspector, Herr Bellau."

"I can't imagine anyone pressuring him."

"There are ways, if you have information. He is not to be trusted, but then, who is? He was most useful. We traced you in a shipment of theatrical goods to Alexandria, and then by lorry across the Nile and then south to here. We

95

lost you for a day or so, and then used our charts to eliminate all possible drop-points where they might be hiding you. And so we finally came here."

"Does the Egyptian government know all this?"

"Nothing at all. There has not been the slightest ripple of interest in official circles yet, according to our informants. I told you, when it comes to a question of our freedom—no, more than freedom, our lives and our country, we go to any extreme of danger and risk. The results are sometimes quite effective."

"Then Cairo isn't in on this?"

"Nasser long ago declared Selim El-Raschid a stinking dog and an enemy of all Islam and Arab peoples." Asche spoke wryly. "On the other hand, since he is such a weathercock between East and West, we can hardly appeal to the Egyptians for help, can we?"

"All right. Get up. How long were you following us? And why did you watch us for so long?"

"I wasn't sure what you were up to. You might have been part of a trap, set by the Dancers."

"You mean you still don't trust me."

Asche said coldly: "And should I?"

Durell smiled. "We're in a rotten business, Simon. I suppose we just have to make the best of it."

Simon's equipment was as efficient as promised. He led them a mile south, to a jeep parked behind a dune that followed a macadam road westward. In the jeep were clothes of both Arab and European design. There was also water and sandwiches and a medical kit to dress Durell's arm. Simon was quick at it, glancing now and then at the sky.

"It will soon be light. We're not far from the valley of the Nile, even though you probably felt we were on the surface of the moon. We'll reach the river by dawn."

Durell was content to let him have his way. More than content, he was grateful, for Lisl's sake. She was at the end of her strength, and he knew that if they'd had to spend this day in the desert, she would have been finished.

Simon drove the jeep. It had no muffler, and their progress was noisy. As the light strengthened, they saw increasing vegetation, high palms behind mud walls, then one village and another, noisy with naked, tumbling children infested with sores and covered with flies. Fields of rice suddenly appeared, a startling green after the barren brilliance

96

of the sand dunes. Irrigation ditches led like arrows to the west, where more palm trees were fringed by the light of the rising sun appearing behind them. At the third village, Simon stopped the jeep beside a water wheel, where three men dressed in the traditional burnouses and *chechias* of Bedouin nomads were waiting for them. There were houses with red and orange glass windows, and an odor of filth in the air; scores of children ran shrieking and naked, playing with garbage. The three Bedouins were smoking cigarettes as Simon halted.

"*S'laam,*" one man said.

They looked like three of the most desperate rogues Durell had ever seen, two gaunt ones and one who panted with his fat, but who slung a heavy crate into the back of the jeep as if it were a bag of feathers. He was the leader, one-eyed, with a drooping moustache and beard, an eagle's nose of tremendous proportions, and a mouth as cruel as the slash of a dagger. Simon introduced them casually.

"This is Ibrahim Ben-Haakim," he said, touching the fat, one-eyed man. "His son Josef is one of the first Bedouins to give up the nomad life and attend our University of Jerusalem. He's studying medicine there under a grant from the State of Israel. The Bedouins sorely need their own professional men. If you know them, you will realize what a departure Josef has made from his traditional way of life."

Durell returned the greetings, saying, "Peace," and the fat man touched his forehead and lips gravely.

"Whatever we seem to you outwardly," Ben-Haakim said, "we are friends, and we follow Major Asche wherever he leads us, even into the heart of those who make a sacrilege of Islam."

Simon's eyes flickered. "These men are devout Moslems, Durell. They're not taken in by all the rumors about a new prophet about to take the place of Mohammed. If anything, they hate El-Raschid more than you and I."

The village was astir with dawn life, but none of the fellahin going to their fields paid any attention to the noisy jeep and the Bedouins around it. It was as if they were invisible, Durell thought, and he gave due respect to Simon and his organization. Whatever showy progress had been made in the big cities, this village reflected the same filth and poverty the fellahin had suffered for five thousand years. From the single Arab café came a blare of radio propaganda, and over the ragged awning of reed mats was a faded photograph of Nasser, with a background of militia behind him like a crown of bayonets. Some villagers sat at the café, drinking mineral water, while the flies buzzed, crawled, and clustered in black heaps on the garbage in the street.

In the square, Ben-Haakim's men squatted and brewed tea over a charcoal fire, drinking it from small brass cups with sprigs of mint in it. The men ate and drank quietly, and there was no mingling with the villagers. After half an hour, Simon gave a signal and they all crowded on the jeep.

It was a short trip to the Nile. The green of cultivated fields on each side of the great river valley was startling after the desert glare. At another village, a felucca waited for them at a rickety dock, manned by what seemed to be another quartet of the one-eyed relatives of Ben-Haakim. Now they were out in full view of river traffic, which consisted of more feluccas, steamers, tugs and barges moving up and down the vast stream. An Army convoy in trucks roared by the landing, the troopers in smart berets and khaki uniforms, with arms slung over their shoulders. But no one gave their little group a second glance.

It was a three-hour trip down the river to Cairo. Ben-Haakim gave them food and fresh water, and Lisl curled up on a prayer rug and slept in the shade of the tattered sail. Durell felt the effects of the long days and nights, too; his eyes felt as if sand had scratched them, and he was content to let Simon and his ragamuffin desert friends take charge for the time. Simon seemed unperturbed by the danger of discovery by river patrols. He was lost in thoughts of his own, his broad face ravaged, his intelligent eyes turned inward on vengeful grief. Durell doubted the man's emotional stability. Simon's cold efficiency was unnatural and might yield to a violent explosion in the time ahead that could betray them all.

Cairo had not changed much since Durell's last visit some years ago, but he was impressed by the new urban sprawl, the air of the cosmopolitan business section that shocked one's sense of orientation with a mingling of ancient and medieval Mohammedan culture in bazaars and shops and glittering modernity in hotels and corporate office buildings. When they arrived at noon, the heat had slackened some of the waterfront activity. Two more of Ben-Haakim's tribesmen waited for them, looking like the waterside loafers idly watching the barges that unloaded drums of pesticide and flour. Many of the bags of flour had burst on the dock due to careless handling, and the air was filled with a white haze that settled on everything within a quarter of a mile of the corrugated-tin warehouses.

Simon spoke rapidly to Ben-Haakim, who nodded and gave orders to his followers. In a moment a big Chrysler wheeled up on the dock and Simon, Ben-Haakim, Lisl, and Durell got in behind a uniformed chauffeur.

"Our plane doesn't leave until evening. The reservations are all in order—I was optimistic, you see—and I have British passports for all of us at the hotel, as well as some fresh clothes to make us presentable as tourists. We'll have to fly by way of Athens, of course."

"And our final destination?"

"We are at a dead end here. We'll have to approach from the other direction to get at Raschid."

"Do you know where he is?"

"I can make an educated guess. Ben-Haakim has been a fountain of information for us. As you see, he has no love for upstart prophets, and his people wander freely over the borders of the Middle East." Simon smiled. "It is useful. They are loyal, since the Bedouin and the Druse tribes never quarreled with us, and make up some of our best citizens."

The big limousine moved smoothly through the tangled traffic of metropolitan Cairo. There was the usual din of clanging trolley bells, buses, and taxis, and in the narrower streets, donkeys and foot traffic contesting the way amid a bedlam of hooting, honking and cursing. Along the open bazaars and shops, nearly naked shoeshine boys squatted on their boxes, too lacking in energy to wave away the flies that clustered on their faces. They passed cafés that smelled of urine, stale wine, and hashish smoke, narrowly avoiding a stream of cats darting across the street, then an open rug market where small girls worked at the looms, their henna-stained fingers nimble on the colored threads. They passed the Hilton, near Tahreer Square, and swung into Elhamy Street on the bank of the Nile, with its tall, graceful palms on a green screen of lawn against the busy river. Beyond the Semiramis, which also overlooked the Nile, was the new hotel that was their goal, a glittering glass-and-aluminum tower that looked as if its plaster hadn't yet dried. The chauffeur swung the car smoothly to an elegant side entrance between towering oleanders and traveler palms.

"Here we are," Simon said cheerfully. "A hot bath and fresh clothes will make new people of us all—not to mention new identity papers and passports."

It was strange to have traveled from the savage desert to the luxury of soft carpets, red-jacketed busboys, indirect lighting, and piped Western music all in the space of a few hours. Lisl moaned ruefully and smoothed her heavy blonde hair, then gave it up and tried to carry off her entrance as best she could. The side lobby did not take them directly through the main public rooms, fortunately, and one of the elevators whisked them swiftly up to the fourteenth floor. The operator with his red pillbox cap and gilt-embroidered uniform did not even seem to see them. Simon had prepared the way quite well.

Perhaps too well, Durell thought.

He was not accustomed to putting his life and his chances for success in the hands of another. Because of Lisl, he had been content to let Simon lead them from the desert to safety. But from the moment of the Israeli's appearance, he had waited to take command of his own destiny again.

It was interesting, too, that since they had reached the comparative safety of civilization, Lisl's attitude toward him had changed subtly. In the limousine, as they watched the contrasts of abysmal poverty and glittering wealth, Lisl had tended to pay more attention to Simon.

Simon, too, had regarded her with odd speculation. At one point, before they reached the hotel on Elhamy Street, Simon said: "Carole was fond of you, Lisl. She always hoped to make amends for using you. I trust you can find a way to forgive me, too."

"You did what was necessary," Lisl murmured. "I understand it better now. But you're wrong, you know. I'm sure now that my father is innocent of all the charges that were made against him."

Simon had glanced briefly at Durell. "Does our American friend make that claim?"

"I do," Durell said.

"Perhaps you only wish to salve your American conscience for employing such people. Isn't that possible?"

"I think Hubertus Steigmann is someone you've confused with another," said Durell. "I don't yet know who, or how it happened, but I'm convinced of it."

"Do you say this to get Lisl on your side, Sam?" The

Israeli's dark eyes smiled, but his voice was caustic. "We are allies for the moment. Must we quarrel over this?"

"We don't quarrel," Lisl said. "But neither do you put me on a plane for Europe. Wherever you go, I go, too. I want to find my father."

"So you shall," Simon said. "You remind me, rather painfully, of Carole, you know."

"Painfully?"

He hesitated. "You are very much like her."

Thereafter Simon spoke little, but Durell did not miss the way Lisl stole long, speculative glances at the man's blunt face. Women, he thought with an inner sigh, were never to be understood. Give them a man suffering grief over another woman, and they yield sympathy like melting butter. Lisl might be naïve, but she was very much a woman, and Simon had just flattered her in a manner perhaps intended to win her over to his future needs. But he decided to let time settle the matter. . . .

Now, as they stood outside the door of Simon's suite on the fourteenth floor of Cairo's newest hotel, he determined to take over again.

But it was almost too late.

Simon opened the ornate door with a key and stepped aside to let Lisl enter. Durell held her back.

"Wait. We may have company."

He moved in fast, kicking the door hard inward, then stepping quickly to one side, flat against the wall of the lavish suite, his eyes fanning the big, sunny, air-conditioned room with a quick sweep that focused instantly on the gnome-like figure who sat in a deep armchair, waiting for them.

It was Inspector Franz Bellau.

Chapter Nineteen

SIMON had not expected the dwarf. His blunt face reflected dismay, and a gun jumped like magic into his hard fist. Durell pushed it down with a calm he did not feel.

"You move quite fast, Herr Inspector," he said quietly. "Very fast, and very cleverly."

"Did you not expect me?" Bellau smiled cheerfully. "But it was not too difficult to trace you to Egypt."

"To this hotel? To this room?" Simon demanded.

"My dear Major Asche, we are all of us very clever people, are we not?" Bellau was ingratiating. "We have our information sources, our files on our friends and enemies. How is Ibrahim Ben-Haakim, by the way? I do not see him with you."

Simon swore thickly. Durell closed the door and said: "I think we can all use some food and a tall, cool drink, Simon. Will you call down for something?"

The Israeli said angrily: "But no one could know of our plans, or this suite. Why is this man here? Did you tip him—?"

"How could I?" Durell asked. "Let's not quarrel for the amusement of the Inspector."

"Exactly," said Bellau. He looked as he had been in Munich. His round, gnome's head was still too large for his pipe-stem neck, and his tiny feet, in shining patent-leather shoes, dangled several inches from the floor as he sat at ease in the big chair. He wore what seemed to be the same theatrical, flowing ascot of blue polka-dots. His antique walking stick with its gold knob supported his chin, and only the yellow tiger's eyes betrayed the real danger in the man as he considered Durell, Asche and the girl. "We must not quarrel," he said. "We have one goal in common, *nein*? We all seek the Second Prophet and his crew of murderous Dancers, and whatever else we do *not* have in common, we surely have this. My files on Major Asche are quite complete, and include his Bedouin friends and his apparatus here in Cairo. I put one and two together"—he nodded to Asche, then to Durell and Lisl—"and came here to wait for your arrival. I must congratulate you on your success to this point."

"What do you want?" Durell asked bluntly.

"Merely to join your effort, as I said. And I must suggest that your presence illegally in Egypt, whose government, like most dictatorships, is paranoiacally suspicious of illegal entries and espionage, is utterly dangerous."

"The security police here are not alerted."

"How can one know?" Bellau asked blandly.

Simon asked angrily: "Did *you* alert them?"

"Please, I told you, we are allies."

"Only because it suits your dirty little schemes, Bellau," Simon said. "We have our dossier on you, too, and not much of it is good."

102

"Did I not cooperate with you in Munich? Is it my fault that Dr. Steigmann escaped our custody?"

Durell said: "I've been thinking about that, and by all the laws of probability, I'd guess it *was* your fault."

"My dear Mr. Durell—"

"Just one moment," Durell said.

The atmosphere of suspicion and anger had built up too rapidly, Durell decided. He smiled, and again told Simon to order food and drinks, and suggested that Lisl take a shower. Simon remembered he had fresh clothes for all of them, and while he produced them, Durell checked the lavish suite with meticulous care. He was always careful, and his reflex alarm bells were clamoring in the back of his mind as he made a swift search of the hotel rooms. There was a bath and bedroom and the sitting room they first entered, with all the windows overlooking Elhamy Street and the rich lawns that swept down to the banks of the Nile. He checked the bath before Lisl, with a timid and grateful smile, edged by, only too anxious to shed her tattered clothing and try on the outfit Simon had procured for her. He found nothing. The bedroom was also clean. There was a small balcony, reached through sliding glass doors, but no one could get on it from those on either hand on the same floor, and those above were staggered so that it would take an extraordinary acrobat to swing from one to another, and then only with the utmost risk. Durell did not count it out, but no one was there, and everything seemed safe.

Bellau watched him as he went about the sitting room, upturning chairs, looking behind the prints on the walls, unscrewing bulbs in the ornate brass lamps, checking under the Persian carpet and testing the ivory inlay of a hexagonal Bombay table. He found nothing, and this struck a wrong note. He respected the Egyptian security apparatus, knowing them to be neither stupid nor careless. Possibly, the listening devices had been installed when the hotel was being built. Very few new buildings in foreign capitals were neglected at that stage by security police. But his uneasiness persisted.

He changed clothes, accepting the dark British-made suit that Simon tossed to him, and put on a fresh cotton shirt with gratitude. The passports Simon produced had authentic photographs of himself and Lisl; they were described as British subjects on a BEA tour of the Near East.

"It's good work, Simon," he admitted. "How long do we stay here?"

"Until after dinner. We shall eat in the suite, and then Ben-Haakim will drive us to the airport."

"Then we must wait six hours, at least."

"It cannot be helped," Simon said.

"And what do you propose to do with Bellau?"

Simon shrugged. "Accept him as one of us, I suppose."

"I think not," Durell said flatly.

The tone of his words made the dwarf raise his chin from the golden head of his walking stick. "My dear Durell, you are right to be suspicious, but your suspicions should not be directed at me. The Egyptians also hunt the Dancers, naturally, and they mean to smash this self-styled Second Prophet. Some years ago, the man who was then known as Colonel El-Raschid tried an unsuccessful coup against Nasser and almost succeeded in an assassination attempt, in order to seize political power here. Such matters are not lightly forgotten, and never forgiven, in Cairo. El-Raschid is known for his lust for power and his grandiose schemes to write his name into history. This scheme is already operative, and no doubt has gone successfully beyond its first stages. He has gathered men who share his fanaticism, and he uses religious zeal and frenzy to equate his use of the finest minds on this planet with his own stature. You may rest assured that his danger is recognized here in Egypt."

"And Egypt," Durell said flatly, "also knows the value of the power he's gathered in his hideout, wherever it is. Egyptian security doesn't hunt him for altruistic motives. From the past record, it's a moot point as to which hands may prove most dangerous, given this power. Nasser wouldn't lightly give up the men and devices that El-Raschid has stolen."

Bellau sighed gently and considered his elegant walking stick. "You must learn to trust Simon."

"I do trust him. But I don't trust you. I have the feeling we're being listened to, and I also have the feeling that you made this long trip to satisfy your greed for information, Inspector Bellau, which you can use in your notorious files that have saved your skin so often in the past. What do you want from us?"

"Like all Americans, you are blunt. But I do prefer honesty. It is refreshing, I must say, in our business."

"What do you want?" Durell insisted.

"Everything you know, all that you have learned in these

past few days." Bellau's yellow tiger's eyes glistened. "After all, I may prove to be helpful."

"I doubt that. And if we don't share what we know?"

Bellau rubbed his chin with the gold head of his stick. "Are you proposing a bargain?"

"I'm asking what you hold over us as blackmail. What if we just kick you out of here and tell you to go about your business?"

"Then I should be forced to do just that."

"Meaning—?"

"One call to the Egyptian security office here and none of you will ever board that plane tonight."

Simon Asche growled angrily in his bull's throat. In the bathroom, the long hiss of Lisl's shower finally ended. It was quiet then. Durell moved with care to the center of the room, facing the exquisite little man.

"Bellau, you haven't been honest with us from the start, even though you say honesty is refreshing. Let's have some clean air in here. You have files on Dr. Steigmann that could give us the truth about him. Lisl is risking her life to learn that truth. You know whether Steigmann is innocent or guilty of war crimes. Give us the answer now."

"I am sorry; that is not possible."

"Simon?" Durell said.

Simon nodded and moved to the other side of the dwarf's chair. The round head came about to survey both men. Bellau leaned on his stick and slid his tiny feet to the floor.

"I seem to be surrounded. I do not like threats, gentlemen. I'm afraid all deals are now off."

"Yes, they are," Durell said. "Especially since you've been betraying us from the moment we came in here."

"I do not understand."

"Give me your stick, Inspector."

"My stick?"

"Your pretense of stupidity· is foolish. And we know you're not a fool, only a self-seeking egotist balancing your life on a pile of secret dossiers that give you extraordinary power, both East and West. Give me the stick."

Bellau started his move, and he was fast, but Durell was faster. As the dwarf drew back on the gold head of the cane, exposing a flash of steel from the hidden sword inside, Durell jumped and caught his wrist and wrenched hard. Bellau was surprisingly strong, but he lacked the weight to counter Durell's leverage. He cried out something that was

105

not in German, but Arabic; he tried to lunge away, twisting the long tongue of steel out of Durell's grip and slashing the air before him with swift, whipping gestures that could have been murderous. Lisl cried out in alarm, and Durell leaped over the chair to take Bellau from the side. The sharp tip of the sword-cane hissed dangerously near as Bellau backed for the door. Durell came in under his guard at the same moment that Simon struck from the other side. The sword went spinning in a deadly arc across the room. Bellau gave a high-pitched yelp and tried to evade Durell's grip. But Durell picked him up and slammed him without ceremony into the deep armchair. The little German bounced, tried to rise, and looked into the muzzle of Simon's gun, and then into Durell's equally deadly blue eyes.

"Enough," Bellau gasped. *"Bitte.* I yield!"

Durell let out a long breath and picked up the gold-handled sheath of the sword. "It isn't the steel I'm worried about, Bellau. It's your transmitting radio."

He wrenched at the golden griffin head on the cane and unscrewed it swiftly, exposing a tiny broadcasting outfit that hummed when he put it to his ear. Small wonder he'd found no microphones in the suite! From the moment of their arrival, Bellau had been broadcasting every word they had spoken! But to whom? And where?

Simon's breath exploded in a gust of anger. "The little swine has betrayed us. Let me kill him, Sam."

"One moment."

"We cannot let him live!"

"We can't let him die, either, Simon." Durell surveyed the gnome gravely. "Tell us about Steigmann, quickly."

Bellau's face had turned a pasty gray with fear. His yellow eyes were bloodshot, jerking from one ominous figure to the other. "There were two Steigmanns—brothers—very close in age and appearance. One was in charge of a prison camp, an SS colonel as well as a scientist, and the other specialized in optics and electronics. Both brilliant men. We know that one was killed. The other made it to the West in safety and was employed by the AMG. But which one? I still do not know."

Durell said thinly: "This is no time for lies. Which was innocent?"

"I swear, it is all confused, and I would like to know the truth myself!"

Durell glanced at Lisl and saw the sudden hope flicker

106

across her tense face. He nodded briefly. "All right, we'll drop it for now. Who was at the other end of your little broadcasting system?"

Bellau was silent.

Simon said: "I'll give the swine five seconds. One—two—three—"

Bellau spread his small hands in a defensive gesture as if to push away Simon's threat. "Wait, I know when I am defeated. I have my own people here in Cairo—"

"You're sure it wasn't the Egyptians?"

"They cooperate with us, but I was not yet ready to advise them of what I know."

"If you're lying and we're caught," Durell said decisively, "you'll die first, do you understand?"

"I am not lying."

"Then let's get out of here. Simon, can you get Ben-Haakim?"

"He is downstairs in the lobby."

"Get the car. We'll have to change our hideout."

"And Bellau?"

"We take him along." Durell looked angrily at the dwarf. "We'll use him as hostage for a safe passage."

Chapter Twenty

THE ROOM was small and smelled of stale food, sweat, urine, and dust. Inspector Bellau protested with fastidious distaste when Ben-Haakim led them through a crowded rug bazaar and the back rooms of phony-antique merchants who seemed to close their eyes to their presence. Through the small, barred windows of the room came the clanging of trolley bells and auto traffic as the shops reopened after their one-o'clock pause in the heat of the day. Ben-Haakim, fat and sweaty, brought them couscous and water in mineral flasks and handed Durell a bottle of American bourbon with a small, knowing smile on his villainous face. Durell accepted it gratefully, not surprised that the Bedouin knew his personal taste; Simon would have briefed him long ago.

He sat with his back to the wall, watching the others through the weary hours of the afternoon, and tried not to feel trapped by their circumstances. He had done what he could. It was not Simon's fault that Bellau had wrecked their escape plan. But he felt impatient to get on with it, knowing it was more necessary than ever to recover Professor Steigmann and clean up the Dancers.

Lisl and Simon talked together in low whispers for endless hours. He could tell by the girl's soft and gentle face that Carole Bainbury was one topic of discussion, and their own problems another. He felt rueful about their intimacy. Yesterday, Lisl had depended on him for every move; today, all her interest was centered on the Israeli agent. Not that she was fickle—and even if she were, it would be a matter of relief to him not to be responsible for her. But she was like a lost child, trying to find her way home where she could know herself and feel safe and have a purpose that had not existed before. On the other hand, he was pleased that Simon's eyes had lost their dead bleakness, and showed some flickers of animation as he talked to the girl. Durell sighed. He was not in the business as a matchmaker. None of it would matter if they did not escape from Cairo tonight. . . .

At dusk, the one-eyed Ben-Haakim appeared with two of his tribesmen. He reported the city quiet, with no unusual police activity. Bellau seemed relieved. He insisted that his game with the radio transmitter had been only to relay information to one of his personal aides in his Cairo apparatus. But it still remained to be seen, Durell thought, who really had been listening and what action might follow.

A different car was used to take them through the streets of Cairo to the airport. Lisl sat next to Durell. She was silent, but her eyes kept watching Simon. Noise and lights flashed by in dizzy patterns. Ben-Haakim had given them all new arms, but Durell wondered about the validity of the passports Simon had provided. He studied Bellau, whose reputation as a baleful spider sitting amidst his secret microfilmed records was known to every espionage agency in the world. Surely Bellau knew his life was at stake, if he were lying. Would he run such a desperate bluff, if his radio had contacted only his own people, and they tried to pull him free at the airport? Durell did not know. The dwarf's face gave nothing away.

It was easy, after all. Perhaps too easy. His suspicion never faded as they entered the air terminal and waited for their BEA flight to Athens. The airport was crowded with all the colorful costumes and variety of faces of the Near East. The noisy babble never relented. And yet the Egyptian customs scarcely glanced at their papers as they filed aboard the waiting jet. It was not until they were airborne that Durell permitted himself to relax. He noted with wry amusement that Lisl maneuvered herself into a seat beside Simon Asche. Bellau did not struggle against Durell's gun in his back. He did not create a scene about his forcible "abduction."

But Simon protested with quiet anger. "Why take him with us? The creature is better off dead, as far as we are concerned."

"He can still be useful," Durell said.

"What can he know? If we try for the Dancer hideout from the Negev, he may betray us again."

"Have you pinpointed this hideout, Simon?"

Simon shrugged. "Judging from where they took you, we can conclude it is somewhere in the Sinai Desert. It is a rocky wilderness, of course, but Ben-Haakim's people know it well. He will meet us at the camp where we've been digging in the Nabatean ruins. It's a perfect cover. He'll have the help and information we need."

Durell went along with it. He had reached the same conclusions himself, and was not about to give up at this point. But from what he knew of the Sinai, it was a vast, tortured area of flinty mountains, without roads, settlements, water, or food.

The prospects of digging El-Raschid out of there seemed rather slim.

Athens was a brief reminder of turbulent glory, a glimpse of the floodlighted Acropolis from the air, and contact at last with a K Section resident. Mike Xanakias * met Durell ten minutes after receiving his call from an airport booth. He was a dark, vital man whose whole being seemed to strain at the problem with single-minded purpose. He took Durell's report on the Dancers on a portable tape recorder and promised to send it at once by scrambler to Washington.

"Bellau must have been telling the truth in Cairo, then," Xanakias said. "He was only relaying information to his own

*See *Assignment—The Girl in the Gondola*

people, and perhaps the Gehlen Bureau he nominally works for near Munich. Will they interfere?"

"I don't know. We'll wait and see."

"And you, Cajun? You go on with these people?"

"There's no other way to get at the Prophet."

"But they are dangerous company. I can arrange to put another man on it with you."

"Thanks, Mike. No. Don't look so worried."

"Geneva Central raised hell when you vanished in Munich. They wanted to spot your movements along the Dancer railway."

Durell grinned. "Well, I happened to get on a dead-end line, it seems. We'll have to tackle it from another direction now. And I think we've pulled Bellau's teeth. I want him with me because I've got a lot of pumping to do at that well, before he goes dry."

Mike Xanakias looked at him with mournful Greek eyes and hurried off to send Durell's report on to Washington.

They took an El Al jet to Tel Aviv from Athens within the hour, and landed in Israel shortly after midnight. They were in Simon's territory now, and Major Asche took over with harsh efficiency. Lisl looked disappointed when Simon hurried them into a car and directed the military driver to take the coastal road south, away from the shining new city.

"I'd hoped to see what was being done here," she murmured. "I've always wanted to see this land of new hope and courage—"

"There will be time later, I hope," Simon said. His smile had something softer in it than his previous melancholy. "Ben-Haakim cannot possibly reach our Negev camp before tomorrow night, going overland, but I think that time is running short for us."

Throughout the trip, Inspector Bellau maintained a sullen, gnomish silence. He was a prisoner, in one sense, since he was constantly covered either by Durell or Simon, who took turns at staying alert for any trickery. On the other hand, once they were free of Cairo, it was clear he could do no damage for the time. There was some weight to his protests of innocence, since he seemed willing enough to accompany them.

"We may not trust each other, Herr Durell," he said, breaking his silence in the car that sped south from Tel

Aviv through the warm autumn night. "But we must accommodate one another, *nein?* Our interests merge into a common goal."

"That depends on how much you can remember from your famous files on Dr. Hubertus Steigmann."

"But I have already explained the situation."

"I don't believe you, and never shall."

"My dear Herr Durell, we are both policemen, in a sense, hunting down international criminals—"

"True, but we have different ends. Yours is to fatten your personal files, to keep your skin in one piece." Durell looked at the dwarf's shadowed face in the darkness of the car. "I'd give something to know what *your* background of activity has been since 1939."

Bellau's yellow eyes blazed with anger for a moment, then he relapsed into silence while the car sped south along the shore of the Mediterranean Sea.

Lisl was nodding and trying desperately to keep awake when they entered the narrow, twisting streets of the Israeli sector of Jerusalem. Durell was also feeling the effects of their long imprisonment in the desert hut, the abrupt trip to Cairo, the tension of their escape with Bellau, and the disorienting air flights to Greece and back to the eastern shores of the Mediterranean. The nightmare hours in the hut seemed endless in retrospect, and since then they had been constantly on the move, always alert for danger. He looked at Lisl with sympathy and agreed with Asche when the Israeli major suggested a brief halt at a small, relatively obscure hotel to wash up, eat, and perhaps rest for a few hours. Durell nodded. Perhaps Simon had his own motives for halting here, since this was Simon's home ground, and it was plain that he commanded both respect and the heavy arm of police power in the place. Simon had his own ax to grind, too. But who didn't? he thought wearily. He agreed to the rest halt without much debate.

The early morning hours were cool, and the tumbled mass of the Holy City slept under a serene and starlit sky. Far off on the Jordanian side of the Mandelbaum Gate there sounded a brief trumpet and then the clatter and grind of an armored car doing its endless patrol of the armistice line. It was a peace that was not peace, an armed pause for breath, a suspicious watching and waiting, suspicion and anger and jealous scrutiny on both sides of the line. Durell

111

stood at the window in his hotel room and stared for a long time over the tumbled roofs, the rounded mosques, the synagogues and the modern symmetry of the Hebrew University on its hill. A handful of feudal desert monarchs, hand in glove with demagogues who fanned hatred as a means to gain private power, kept this long-tortured land in a turmoil. The Israelis would never yield; the blood of millions of martyrs had taught them to steel their purpose. No threats of being driven into the sea frightened them. And far to the south, along Gaza and the Negev frontier, was a slim patrol of U.N. peace-keepers. They would have to be reckoned with tomorrow, Durell decided, to avoid detection of his illicit probe over the line into Sinai.

But he decided to let tomorrow's troubles take care of themselves. Lisl was safe in her room, and Simon had taken the watch over Bellau, sharing a room with the dwarf while men came and went with reports for Major Asche; and Simon, transformed into a chunky administrative machine, kept his telephone busy with calls both to the north and south of his threatened little country.

There was nothing more Durell could do.

With a last yawn, he dropped into the soft bed and fell instantly into a deep and mindless sleep.

He awoke to the sound of trucks moving into the courtyard behind the little hotel. Simon's bull voice could be heard, giving decisive orders. Durell showered and changed into the new clothing he found provided for him. There were desert boots and khakis and a cloth sun-hat somewhat like those once favored by the old French Foreign Legion. He tapped on Lisl's wall and heard her voice in query, then went into the corridor to join her for breakfast on a small terrace that overlooked the fabled hills of Jerusalem. It was a hot, cloudless day, relieved by a slight breeze from the east.

Lisl looked refreshed and lovely. She flushed faintly as Durell came to join her, and fussed with the breakfast dishes on the little metal table under a blue-and-white striped awning. She, too, had put on desert clothing: fine leather boots and fawn riding pants and a plain white shirt open at her soft throat.

"Relax," he told her gently. "We're quite safe here. For you, the nightmare is over."

"No, it is not. Not until I find Father, and make amends for the terrible things I've done to him. His face haunts me,

112

Sam. I keep seeing how he looked when I refused to listen to him, after he risked everything to see me." She paused. "But it isn't that, after all."

"Are you thinking of our nights in the hut?"

She bit her lip. "I don't know how you regard me, or what it meant to you, but to me it's like a dream, and some of it was wonderful—with you, I mean—but the rest of it—" She shuddered. "I can't imagine what you think of me, Sam."

"I think you expected to die, and what we did was understandable. But if you want to forget it, Lisl—"

She toyed with her scrambled eggs, and spoke in a small voice. "Have you told Simon about us?"

"Of course not." He kissed her uncertain mouth. "And you seem interested in Simon."

"Yes, I am."

"You should examine your motives carefully, Lisl. Don't just make him into another cause by which to make amends for German guilt. Simon would reject that."

"I know. I've thought about it most of the night. He's different from other men. He's dedicated to the future here, to building something fine and decent for generations to come, to defend the land and develop it. It's a wonderful thing to find today. He's a soldier, educator, scholar—and yet he can move into your world of war and intrigue without any loss of all his fine, sensitive qualities."

Durell laughed softly. "This has hit you very suddenly, Lisl."

"Yes, it has. As for you and me, I'm sorry—"

He did not hurt her by showing relief at being freed of his responsibility for her. "You are unforgettable, Lisl, and it was a rare thing in my life. But I suppose I can't measure up to Simon in your life. I understand how you must feel."

"Do you really, Sam? If so, I'm most grateful."

He patted her hand. "Don't trouble yourself about it. I only hope you can help ease Simon's grief over Carole."

"Oh, I hope so," she said earnestly. "I want to do that, very much."

They joined Simon in the courtyard. A small convoy had been collected, three jeeps and a stake body truck, loaded with archaeological equipment: tents, tools, crates of books, cameras, cases of food. Simon's military training was evident in the efficient way the little convoy was organized.

He greeted Lisl with a smile that warmed the severity of his harsh face. "You both slept well?"

Durell nodded. "When do we leave?"

"In two hours. We're waiting for some equipment from the University. It does not matter, since we cannot look for Ben-Haakim to cross the Sinai before tomorrow, at the very earliest. We can study some aerial maps I have with me, to plan our searches." He regarded Lisl with surprised interest. "You look well. A good night's rest and new clothes always work wonders for a woman's morale."

There were shadows under Simon's deep brown eyes. Lisl quickly asked if he could not find time to take her about the ancient city, and Durell was not surprised when Simon agreed. He stood aside and begged off when Simon asked if he would like to accompany them, but took a pass from Simon to enable him to move about freely. After they drove off, he returned to his room and used the telephone to call the number of an Israeli philatelist who served as a political analyst for K Section. The CIA man, a Mr. Herschel, had facilities for sending coded microdot messages to Washington on canceled postage stamp specimens. He sounded relieved when Durell identified himself.

"I've been sitting on an 'Urgent' from Annapolis Street since dawn," the agent said. "The General has word of an impending crisis. He thinks your activities have alarmed the Dancers to the point where they may make their first strike. If they do, he believes the entire Middle East may blow up. Washington has tentatively warned the Israeli government to expect trouble. Another warning has gone to the Arab states to respect the U.N. truce lines. But of course, none of this will affect El-Raschid. That madman does not care what he destroys with his stolen toys and kidnapped brains, eh? Not as long as he inflames all Islam into a new, holy war against Western infidels."

"Are there any specific orders for me?" Durell asked.

"Yes. You are to proceed immediately, at all risks, to find and destroy the headquarters of the Second Prophet."

Durell thanked him wryly and hung up.

Chapter Twenty-one

"ONCE there were rivers in this desert," Simon Asche said, unconsciously taking on the air of a lecturer. "Ben-Gurion once announced that here in the Negev stood the cradle of our ancient people. The Negev is both the hope of our nation and our weak point and danger zone. What the ancient Nabateans accomplished here, with engineering works that brought irrigating waters to this wasteland, we hope to do, too. We dig here to learn the secrets of those long-dead people, and perhaps to do as they did. If you know the Old Testament, you may recall Isaiah's prophecy."

Durell nodded. " 'And the desert shall rejoice, and blossom as the rose.' Isaiah 35:1."

Simon was pleased. "Exactly. All this was once fertile with vineyards and grain, supporting almost a million people. With modern methods and machinery, we can easily duplicate and surpass what the Nabateans did, despite the waste and erosion of three thousand years of Arab neglect. Water from the Jordan, already on its way through pipelines, will perform the miracle we need."

"All the miracles are human," Lisl said. "All that's being done is with the mind and energy of ordinary people; and yet you are not ordinary, Simon. Your dedication and hope is not an ordinary thing in our world today." She considered the landscape that surrounded the little camp at the head of a long wadi that reached south and east toward the distant frontier. "But it all seems so hopeless. The land is so bleak and empty!"

"We will change it," Simon said. "Give us a chance, and we will make our modern miracles."

At a glance, Durell thought, if you ignored the spirit that moved the men and women in this land, you would say it was a hopeless dream. The land was utterly hostile. In every direction from the camp, with its black Bedouin tents and cook fires, its plank shacks for storage of tools and artifacts, there was nothing but a blinding, flinty emptiness. Jagged peaks rose to the south across the Sinai, and the brazen sun in a copper sky touched a vista of browns and grays with-

115

out a single spot of blessed green to relieve the aching eye and desolate mind. The camp was sheltered by a towering granite cliff behind them, and though it was late afternoon, the sun still struck like a giant fist, and the air in their lungs was like that from the maw of a blast furnace. Simon went on to describe the spring rains that came down in torrential storms that swept the desert, only to be lost in the rocky gullies and sand pools along the seasonal watercourses. But the ancients had managed their irrigation by building low stone dams to form terraced catch-basins along the wadi, and by this means the spring rain was caught and stored for careful use during the growing season. Little remained of that antiquated system of dams now, and even less of the Nabateans who had lived and farmed this incredible land. But the old water-courses had been charted by aerial surveys and foot exploration, and Simon exhibited a map of the area to show how cleverly the features of the land had been exploited.

Aside from the Bedouin workmen, no other human had come into sight through the shimmering, illusory horizon, although Simon mentioned a nomad trail ten miles south where the Arabs, ignoring the artificial boundary of the Egyptian Sinai, casually crossed back and forth with their flocks of sheep, goats and camels, their black-veiled women and half-naked children. Smuggling was still their major occupation, although Simon explained that the Israeli government had experimented with permanent settlements for them and offered schools, medical service, and farms for the youths who could break the nomadic and traditional habits of their desert life.

The Bedouins were silent men when Durell or Lisl stood nearby, but in their black tents could be heard the chatter of women, the tumbling cries of children. Ben-Haakim's men were tall and fierce of eye, with the far look of those accustomed to limitless horizons. The ancient dam they were uncovering yielded to the willing labor of their picks and shovels and the aid of a small bulldozer that by some marvel of heroic labor had been transported to the dig.

Durell was next to Lisl's little hut, which had been Carole Bainbury's during her past year's work here.

"You don't mind?" Simon asked her anxiously.

"Of course not. I only wish I had the training to be as helpful to you as Carole was."

"Don't worry about that," he reassured her. "There's

116

enough to do to oversee the commissary and supervise the general sanitation in the camp."

"I'll be glad to do that. But I'd like to share in the actual work—"

"I'll brief you later on what we're doing." Simon smiled freely for the first time. "I'll make you my private pupil, when we have time."

"I'd like that," she murmured.

At that moment, Durell was more interested in the sound of a distant jet that moved invisibly across the southern horizon. The boom of its engines shook the brazen sky, making a distant growl like that of a threatening beast. He used Simon's field glasses to search out the plane, but could not find it. Then he spotted the thin contrail high above the setting sun. Was it an Egyptian patrol? An Israeli Mystere? Or could El-Raschid have planes of his own? The warning from Washington had been urgent. Somewhere beyond the jagged horizon in the Sinai was a dread destructive force. Infinite terror was brewing there, pushed into a panic by his recent efforts.

He was worried, too, about the failure of Ben-Haakim to appear across the frontier. That fat but competent nomad should be able to take care of himself, but the dangers of crossing the Sinai by illegal routes, where sand filled the water holes and famine was the rule, could not be ignored. These nomads knew the desert as he knew the streets of New York, but there was always the possibility that Ben-Haakim had been lost or worse, perhaps captured either by Egyptian patrols or the fanatic Dancers.

When night fell, only the hissing of gasoline lanterns in the Arab tents offered a reply to his questions. The desert was silent, as cold as a corpse. But something was out there, Durell thought—a thing both malignant and patient, waiting for him.

Twice during the night he awoke to hear the distant thunder of more jets in the dark canopy over the desert. He slept fitfully, dreaming of searing beams of light that made the desert sun seem like a feeble, flickering candle—light that destroyed and ravaged innocent cities and people, licking into flames all the fruit of housing, orchards and vineyards built with the sweat and blood of desperate people. And it would not end there. Religious fanaticism, catching the fire, could sweep the earth with another flame, in which power-mad meddlers would seek their own ends at the cost of millions of lives. The precarious balance of peace in the world would be tipped toward ultimate destruction. . . .

He awoke to a sharp, urgent rap on his tent pole, and heard the canvas pulled aside even as he rolled over on the sleeping pad and reached for his gun. It was past dawn, and the sunlight was harsh and unrelenting beyond the entrance. Major Asche stood there, legs straddled a bit, an automatic rifle in his big paw.

"Cajun?"

"You should be more careful." Durell lowered his gun. "I've got reflexes I can't always control."

Asche said quickly: "Is Lisl here with you?"

"Of course not. What is it?"

"She is not in her hut."

"You're sure?"

"She is nowhere in the camp."

Durell was awake instantly. He was aware of a quick relief in Asche's face, erasing a hard jealousy which had sprung from the expectation of finding Lisl with him; then it was replaced by a savage anxiety. "Take it easy, Simon. We'll find her."

"But she is gone!"

"Let's see where she slept."

The hut assigned to Lisl had been between his and Simon's quarters. Durell narrowed his eyes against the glare of sunlight. Already heat was splintering off the mica-encrusted cliffs and barrens of the desert. Nothing was to be seen beyond the Bedouins' goatskin tents except tumbled and forbidding emptiness.

Nothing was disturbed in Lisl's quarters. There was no sign of violence, except that her blanket was thrown back in disarray, and her small handbag, a gift from Simon yesterday in Jerusalem, was still there. Durell blew air through pinched nostrils. Perhaps she had only gone for a walk. But even that held its dangers in this wasteland.

"She's not visiting the Arabs in the camp?"

"She has not been seen."

"What about the guards you posted?"

"Not a sound. No alarm."

"What about a search party, in case she simply went exploring?"

"They are looking now."

118

Durell felt a slow dread. "Did you check Herr Bellau? Or has he slept through all this?"

Simon was stunned. "But I put a guard on his hut. If that little dwarf had anything to do with Lisl—"

Durell ran for the Inspector's quarters. When they threw open the door to waken Bellau, they found only the Bedouin guard. The Arab lay sprawled on his back, teeth glittering between surprised lips. A knife had been plunged into his heart. Durell swore, dropped to one knee. The man had been killed some hours ago. Simon's breath hissed in angry dismay.

"They are both gone, then," he whispered.

Durell nodded. "But where?"

The Bedouins went out on foot and camel to scour the rocky wilderness. It must have looked like this to Moses, Durell thought grimly, during his forty years of wandering with the Children of Israel. Two men took the jeep toward the border, ten miles away. Durell accepted a cup of mint tea from the Bedouin cook and watched Simon pace like a caged bear, while a wail of lament lifted from the black tents when the news of the guard's murder reached the Bedouin women.

"They've taken her," Simon gritted. "I should have expected it. Even if Steigmann accepted the Dancers' help out of panic, back in Munich, it's obvious that now he is an unwilling prisoner, and they need Lisl to make him talk. They snatched her once. Why not again?"

"But who would know we're here?"

"How do they know anything?" Simon exploded. "They have their spies everywhere, even among us, among the Bedouins."

"And there's been no word from Ben-Haakim?"

"Nothing."

Durell walked to the Bedouin tents and spoke in rapid Arabic to a young, hawk-faced man who turned out to be the son of Sheik Ben-Haakim. His name was Josef. He spoke English, Hebrew, and French as well as his tribal tongue, and had studied under a grant from the Israeli government. His manner, as he told this to Durell, was dignified and grave.

"We heard nothing. It was done with great craft and stealth, and it was also done with the willing agreement of the two who have disappeared. Otherwise there would have

119

been an alarm. I will avenge the murder of my brother, who guarded the German, but even so, unless the girl went willingly, or was forced into silence, they could not have escaped."

"Lisl Steigmann did not go willingly."

"It must have been so," Josef insisted. "But we will soon know the truth." His intense eyes were darkly brooding. "The other alternative is that some of my people are not to be trusted. One cannot know. Some are gullible and greedy, and in a ferment over the religious frenzy that has seized some of the Bedouins, to my shame. The coming of a new Prophet seems to them a time for glory and adventure, as in the old days, and a renewal of our ancient greatness."

"Do you really believe in the Second Prophet?"

"Of course not. I know that El-Raschid is an adventurer, perhaps a madman, but more crafty and dangerous than one might imagine. His influence keeps spreading." Josef eyed him with speculation. "Major Asche is going on a search party himself. We leave in five minutes. Can you ride a camel?"

Durell nodded. "I've managed before."

"These are racing camels. We have only three. Major Asche will use one, and I will ride another. If you wish, you may have the third. We will search the Southern Quarter. It is a very bad land, cursed by Allah since the days the world began."

"Did your father, Ben-Haakim, ever give you a hint as to where he thought El-Raschid might have his headquarters?"

"Never, Mr. Durell. We will have to put our faith in Allah to lead us safely through this day."

Durell respected Josef's sincerity but preferred to put his trust in solid weapons against the Prophet and his crew of fanatics. He decided it was no time to withhold what he knew and walked back to Simon, who was supervising the loading of the water bags on the three camels. The sun struck at the back of his neck like the blow of a fist. Some of the Bedouins had gone to work, following their daily routine, at the Nabatean dam across the flinty wadi. Durell took from his pocket the medallion he had found on the Dancer he'd killed when he escaped from the hut in the desert.

"This is more in your line, Simon," he said. "You're the expert on antiquities in this part of the world. What do you make of this?" The heavy medallion caught the sunlight in the palm of his hand and cast sparkles of hot brilliance in

Simon's angry eyes. Durell had rubbed some of the grime from the engraved surface, and the image of the Dancing Monk was clearly visible, his small foot upraised, his arms lifted, his haloed face touched with a frenzy of joy. He watched Simon's eyes. "Carole had a postcard she intended to give you, back in Munich, with this same figure on it, from a Byzantine mosaic in the museum. Maybe she only learned the name of the 'underground railway' run by the Dancers, and it's obvious that El-Raschid took this motif as a symbol of his movement. Things moved too fast to check it out, but as nearly as I can recall, there was once a sect of monks who lived in the Sinai and believed in a particularly joyous relationship with God, one in which they often danced themselves to exhaustion to express their happiness, which they felt was demanded of them. I know there are still some orthodox monasteries in the Sinai, devoted to Old Testament traditions, and some of them go back over a thousand years in unbroken occupancy."

Simon nodded thoughtfully. "Yes, there are still a few. But the Dancers were supposed to have been extinct for three hundred years or more. They had a monastery on a peak called Djebel Kif, some forty miles over the Egyptian border. I should have thought of this sooner."

"Have you ever seen Djebel Kif?"

Simon shook his head. "Very few men travel that way. It is most inaccessible. The Bedouins think it is accursed by Allah, and I suppose it is one of the most desolate and forbidding places in the world."

"Desolate or not, that's where El-Raschid and his kidnapped crew of scientists must be," Durell decided.

Simon nodded. "If true, it is a prime location to launch surprise attacks either East or West, perhaps in both directions, to begin a war that could touch off flames everywhere. It's the highest peak around—which means that Steigmann's laser beams, if he's perfected a weapon out of them, could reach several capital cities within hundreds of miles of here."

"That's where we go, then," Durell said.

Simon's face was like stone. "You say Carole had learned of all this?"

"Not all of it. Just a hint. What's the matter?"

"Her death is my fault, then," Simon said roughly. "All this trouble, and Lisl's disappearance now—I might have stopped it all some months ago."

"You didn't have this information then. Don't blame yourself so much, Simon."

"I must. First Carole, now Lisl—she's innocent, she doesn't know what we're fighting against."

"I think she does, now."

Simon looked up at him from under frowning brows. "Did you and Lisl—I mean—"

"She's a fine girl," Durell said. "That's all."

Simon straightened. "Yes. Yes, she is. If only we can find her alive."

Chapter Twenty-two

JOSEF ASKED that some of his brethren be taken with them —sturdy desert men whose faces were as flinty as the rocky wasteland into which they proceeded to trail Bellau and the girl. Their camels were not as swift as those Durell and Simon used, but speed was impossible in any case. At first, there was no visible trail in the stone gully that led toward the frontier, but now and then one of Josef's men dismounted and turned over a piece of flint and said something to Ben-Haakim's son. It was an hour before they came to a pool of sand beneath a red escarpment where, in a moment of carelessness, a print had been left.

"They came this way," Josef announced.

"Were they walking?" Durell asked.

"To this point, yes. Just the small man and the young lady."

Simon bit his lip. Either Bellau had persuaded Lisl to come with him voluntarily, as Josef thought, or he had forced her on this mad walk. Durell said: "But not even Bellau would try to walk forty miles across country to Djebel Kif, Simon. He must have arranged a rendezvous with the Dancers close by."

"That means Bellau was always one of the Dancers' men, then," Simon muttered.

Durrell nodded. "Let's get on."

They found the rendezvous point twenty minutes later. Simon announced they had crossed the unmarked Sinai frontier, which meant a ten-mile walk through most of the night for the girl. Durell swore softly in exasperation. How Simon knew the boundary in that trackless wilderness of burning canyons was a mystery. In another stretch of glaring sand amid the red rocks, Josef suddenly urged his camel forward and came upon the tracks of a jeep and the footprints of both Bellau and Lisl and other men. The vehicle tracks swung in a circle and headed southeast toward the jagged peaks on the horizon.

"These are Czech tires," Simon said tightly. "The Egyptian army has some of these machines."

"But the Dancers might have stolen some by raiding a depot," Durell suggested. "I don't think the Egyptians are in this officially, even though they'd like to be."

"What bothers me is how Bellau arranged all this when we had him a prisoner."

"He came willingly," Durell pointed out. "He's not a man to underestimate. In fact, we've done just that, even though we both know how he survived like a cat with nine lives through the war and all the purges. Maybe our little Inspector is more dangerous than El-Raschid, himself. Bellau must have known the Dancer headquarters all along, and got out of our camp with the help of one of Josef's men."

"It will be a cruel day for that one, when Josef finds him out," Simon said grimly.

They pushed on into Sinai territory. The sun whipped them with red-hot flails, and Durell was grateful for the Bedouin burnous that Josef gave him. Progress was an anguish of trial and error, with frequent backtracking and circling of raw, craggy heights that might have been a landscape on the moon. Nothing was to be seen alive here. The only sound was that of the occasional wind that flapped their robes. The camels made an aroma that could be cut with a knife. Now and then sand blew toward them and found its way with uncanny skill into every crevice of the flesh. But for the most part there was only rock, red and gray, looming ahead and behind, to right and left. There was no visible trail that Durell could see, but the Bedouins seemed to know the way.

During a rest halt in the shade of a towering cliff, Durell again heard the distant thunder of a jet. It shook the yellow sky and made sand trickle down the scarp behind them. He drank water sparingly and searched the sky, but he could see no contrail this time. Major Asche urged Josef to press on;

but the Bedouins insisted on the full measure of their mid-morning rest.

When they mounted again, following a desolate valley where they could spot again the jeep tracks, they went only three miles and then Josef pointed to a thin ridge high above them.

"We go that way. The jeep moves faster, but must take a roundabout path. The camels can take us over that cut and save eight miles."

"But we can't catch up with them," Simon protested.

"There was never any hope of that," Josef said. "But we can find where they have gone, and perhaps learn what happened to Ben-Haakim, my father. I search for someone, too, Major. My father is very important to me."

"I'm sorry, Josef. I've been thoughtless."

"I know how you feel about the girl, Major. But it will be as Allah wishes, and no other way, no matter how men seek to change the road of destiny."

Josef's search ended before their own. Two hours of laborious climbing, where they often had to lead the ugly-tempered camels on foot, brought them to the first sign of human habitation, the remains of a Bedouin camp and a well known only to these nomads. The well had been destroyed with an explosive charge and the tents torn into rags. Three bodies sprawled in the blinding sun, and as they approached, there came a flapping of great wings and great, ugly vultures lifted clumsily into the ochre sky and circled resentfully high above the corpses.

The three dead men were Bedouins, and Durell was able to recognize them as Ben-Haakim's people from Cairo. The wind flapped their dark robes open. The vultures had been having a feast. Josef gave a small cry, torn from his stoic throat, and leaped forward to examine the corpses.

"My father?"

But Durell saw that the fat figure of Sheik Ibrahim Ben-Haakim was not among the dead men. At the same moment, the silence was shattered by a crash of a rifle. Durell whirled, saw that one of Josef's men had his gun at his shoulder, and that the target was a dim figure clambering over the crest of the ridge. The figure waved a feeble arm and Durell jumped and knocked away the Bedouin's rifle before he could fire again.

"Hold it!"

Josef stared with narrowed eyes at the man who staggered

124

down the slope toward them. Durell heard the Bedouins suck in their breath at what had almost been done.

"Allah is good," Josef whispered.

"Yes. It's Ben-Haakim, your father."

All of the men belonging to Ben-Haakim had been slaughtered; only the clever, fat sheik had managed to escape. A bullet had creased his scalp, creating a bloody wound that had looked mortal to the Dancers who had ambushed his little caravan at this spot.

"God saw fit to blind those devils to my true condition," Ben-Haakim told them, a few minutes later. Simon was attending to his scalp wound. The fat man panted and grinned at his son and winked his one good eye. "Allah gave us wits to survive; is it a sin to use them if we can? But those devils shall not live long, however clever or strong they are. The True Prophet shall not be denied, and the madmen who defy Allah by proclaiming a new son to Him will meet a satisfactory end, I promise you."

"Are you sure it was the Dancers?" Durell asked.

The fat man grunted. "They waited like thieves in the night. We were careful, but this is their land, and they know it well. We pushed on too quickly, against my better judgment, may Allah forgive me. And so we were sleepy and tired and not as watchful as we should have been. But Allah will grant Paradise to these poor men who died here."

"Do you know Djebel Kif?" Durell asked.

The fat man grinned and nodded his head. "For an American, I can see that you are clever enough. You have learned of the devil's home without me."

"Were you there?"

"We went near enough. But it is hopeless."

"Nothing is hopeless," Simon insisted.

"Then we will go to Djebel Kif and you may see for yourself. No man can go up there who is not wanted. Not even an army."

Durell said: "Maybe so, but there's a way around that, because *I* am wanted by El-Raschid. So I will go up there."

125

DJEBEL KIF loomed against the yellow sky like the true home of Ben-Haakim's Shaitan. They reached it on the afternoon of their second day across the Sinai. The dead men had been buried, and Ben-Haakim, rested and fed, seemed as good as ever. That morning they crossed a military road that twisted through the ominous landscape, but no one was sighted, and Josef's scouts reported no watchers following their progress.

They halted in the shadow of a canyon wall and stared ahead at the bulk of Djebel Kif, a black pillar of basaltic stone that soared above the tumbled crags about them. On the very summit, like a medieval citadel, stood the ruins of the old Byzantine monastery, with foundations sheer against the steep cliffside. There was only a collapsed dome, an arcade, a few stretches of crenellated and buttressed walls against the hot sky. Nothing stirred up there. The desert wind blew stinging sand in their faces as they silently studied the stronghold. Then Ben-Haakim murmured:

"Do not be deceived. It looks deserted, but it is filled with men and machines. Some Bedouins wandered up there last month in search of water, hoping the spring still yielded to the ancient well. But only one man came back, and everyone took him as struck by the madness of the sun, from his tales. When I heard of this, as we came toward you from the Nile, I looked for this man, but I was told he had been murdered. All I could learn was that he never stopped babbling about the devils who haunt Djebel Kif."

Simon Asche was doubtful. "And how does anyone get up there, Ibrahim?"

"There is a road to the south, out of sight. It is the only way up the cliff, and it is well guarded."

"How do they get supplies up there?" Durell asked.

"They are transported first by regular plane to a landing place east of here, and then taken by helicopter to the peak," Ben-Haakim said.

Simon shook his head. "From that peak, they can spot a fly ten miles away. We can't get up unseen. But perhaps an

Israeli army raid across the border—a quick stab and attack, and then retirement across the frontier—"

"We have no time for that. Bellau and Lisl are up there," Durell said. "Something critical is brewing, for El-Raschid to move so boldly."

"I cannot permit you to go up there alone."

"There's no other way," Durell insisted. "El-Raschid wants me, for what I know, and seems to think he might recruit me into his services." He smiled grimly. "I think I'll just let him take me prisoner."

"And then?"

"Then I'll have to play it by ear."

"It is death," Ben-Haakim said gravely. "You are a brave man, but your foolishness may be an affront to Allah." The one-eyed man paused, frowning. "It is said there are secret ways into this mountain, this home of Shaitan, from down below. No man of our tribe ever came here, thinking this is an accursed place, as it truly is. But perhaps we can find the entrance tonight, when it is dark, and reach you, Mr. Durell."

Durell nodded. He liked this fat rogue and his straight young son, and all of Josef's brethren. Simon still protested that it was his responsibility, since he should have taken better care of Lisl, but Durell cut him off.

"I'm counting on you to bail me out of that vulture's nest, if I can't escape myself."

"When will you go?"

"Right now. We haven't much time. If all our theories are correct, El-Raschid may make his move at any moment."

An hour later, he walked around the base of Djebel Kif. Simon and his Bedouins were hidden two miles behind him. The sun burned with stubborn vengeance, a great red ball in the west that seemed to increase its furious assault on his senses as it sank below the jagged horizon. The wind blew grit into his eyes and nostrils, and he used his burnous to keep its choking thickness from his throat.

Nothing stirred in the ruins high above. No animal, bird, or insect sounded; no blade of grass gave relief to the rocky shale under his booted feet.

He had never felt lonelier.

Always before, however solitary his mission, he had been among people, in places built and traversed by man. Now he felt small and helpless in this emptiness that oppressed the soul and sent fingers of unreasoning fear into his mind. He was not at all as confident as he had sounded to Simon when he insisted that El-Raschid would accept him, alive, into that strange stronghold high above. What terror waited for him up there? But somehow in that grim fastness was Dr. Steigmann, with his knowledge of new and deadly weaponry, and scores of other men missing from the normal world these past few months.

This was the end of the underground railway he had been sent to travel. Madness and egomaniacal power waited for him on that windswept crag. It could not be permitted to flourish and perpetrate crimes against humanity.

He walked on.

The opposite slopes of Djebel Kif were not as sheer as those they had faced from the north, and now at last he saw the path, little more than a goat run, squirming and doubling upon itself in its climb to the summit. Less than an hour of daylight remained when he reached its base and paused.

He knew that careful eyes watched him, although he could not locate them, and little bristles at the nape of his neck began to prickle with that sixth sense that told him of it. Where were they? He could hear nothing that might betray the Dancer guards. But they were there, looking down on his remote figure as he began his solitary climb.

It seemed endless.

At any moment, he expected to feel the mortal blow of a bullet tearing through his flesh and bone. El-Raschid was unpredictable. His confidence began to ooze away as the shadows darkened and he reached the halfway mark to the top of the mountain.

And still there was no sign of life, no challenge, no attack.

Was Ben-Haakim mistaken? Had they fallen for a false clue in the Byzantine medallion of the Dancing Monks?

He climbed farther.

Now he could see the crumbling ruins clearly in the last flare of sunlight from the west. The sky beyond was alive with desert colors, harsh and ominous. The wind was stronger here, as hot as if from the furnaces of hell. Above, the Byzantine arches of a cloister stood black against the colors of the sky. Part of one tower, perhaps a belfry, still stood here, forming a gateway at the top of the treacherous path he followed. The arched entrance was like a black maw, beckoning to him.

The last hundred yards were the worst. The feeling that he was covered by several weapons, that at any instant he would suffer the instantaneous shock of death, grew stronger. He forced himself to climb faster, heedless of the wind or the uncertain footing. And at last he stood before the arched, crumbling ruin, where blackness darker than any night waited to swallow him.

And a voice said:

"Welcome, Mr. Durell. Welcome, indeed."

He did not allow his relief to show as he walked forward to greet Selim El-Raschid. His brief encounter with the Second Prophet in far-off Munich had made an indelible impression on him, and his memory of this man's magnetic power wasn't false. In this place he wore again his costume of the ancient Caliphate, richly embroidered with gold and glittering with jewels like a magnificent peacock. But the self-styled Prophet needed no decoration to make himself impressive. His towering height and hawk's face dominated and stunted everything else. The impact of his assurance, the shine of malevolent intelligence in his dark eyes, and the confidence with which he waved a brown hand to beckon Durell inside was like a physical blow.

"We have been expecting you at Djebel Kif, Mr. Durell, for as you see, we never underestimated you. We know your value, and welcome you to our ranks."

Two shadows stirred restlessly behind the giant Prophet. The killer hounds. The twin Dancers he had bested back in Munich, and whose straining impatience showed they had not forgotten his insults, were ready to leap and tear him to pieces. El-Raschid checked them with a murmur. Durell did not look at them again.

Durell eased up a bit.

"You came a long way to satisfy your curiosity, Mr. Durell, and survived several trials," El-Raschid said. "I am sure we may have more surprises for you. But you must remember, you are not forgiven for the way you have annoyed me, and there must be suitable punishment which you will accept, I am sure, as a brave and clever man."

"It's not just my curiosity that brought me here," said Durell. "I want Dr. Steigmann and his daughter."

"Indeed? You make demands? Alone, like this?"

"Is Lisl here?"

"Naturally. And my confederate, Herr Bellau. A very

129

clever little man, and most accommodating. Come with me. For the moment, we will postpone our judgment upon you, and ignore your bravado."

The hounds closed in on either side. Durell nodded and stepped forward before they could touch him. There was a stone path through the crumbling, arched entrance, and he saw that the top of Djebel Kif was relatively flat, once he was within the high walls of the monastery. A master of camouflage had concealed the helicopter landing area with paint and netting, and a small two-seater rested there in the shade. There was an old well and a pond and a garden bordered by squat, bulbous stone columns and arches, and El-Raschid led the way, with a thin smile of amusement, toward the vaulted, dusty stones that once held the monastic cells of the Dancing Monks.

Durell walked between the two Dancers, along a narrow stone gallery and down a circular flight of steps worn smooth by a thousand years of sandaled feet, and then they paused before a heavy wooden portal. The light was almost gone from the sky, glimpsed through the broken, timbered roof. Shadows waited ahead. El-Raschid laughed softly.

"You are honored, Mr. Durell, by my personal greeting. It is not for everyone that I come up here. Do you find this place so strange?"

"No stranger than your dreams of immortality as a Second Prophet."

"But stranger than anything you have seen before, I promise you. We are self-sufficient and impregnable here, beyond reach of any power to obstruct us. Please go in."

The hawk's face was mocking and amused. One of the twin guards opened the wooden door set in the crumbling wall. And when Durell walked through, it was like entering another world, a world of Sindbad, and the Thousand and One Nights, of Omar Khayyam, of Baghdad and all its fabulous wonders.

The mountain was honeycombed with cells and passages under the monastery ruins. Soft lights and a sweep of cool, air-conditioned air indicated a power source that El-Raschid quietly identified as a small atomic reactor, built by German and Egyptian technicians who had joined the Dancer cause. How many hours of man-killing labor, Durell thought, had gone into the embellishment of natural caves in this volcanic mass of stone! The walls were tiled in Moorish patterns, with blues and pinks and antique designs that rivaled the finest mosques of Istanbul. Soft Persian carpets muffled their steps. Then an elevator, with a golden fretwork like that of a giant birdcage, whisked them gently downward for an incalculable distance. He made no move to resist when the hounds searched him, but they neglected to check the hollow heels of his shoes. His only resource was the small tube of nerve gas cached in his left heel. He had small hope it would remain undiscovered for long. And as the elevator sank downward, his hope for success in this place sank alarmingly with it. The elevator seemed to be the only way in or out of this devil's eyrie, and when they stepped from its golden embrace, it was as if they were in another world.

There was intense activity in the corridors and rooms they passed. He glimpsed men in white smocks at work in mysterious laboratories, the costumed Dancers with their scimitars were everywhere, and then, to his shocked surprise, they came face to face with Mademoiselle Zuzu, of the Munich pavilion.

Durell halted.

"Hello, there."

She looked different, but he was certain she was the same girl who had stabbed the needle into the back of his neck at the *Oktoberfest*. She wore a plain blue cotton smock that offered tantalizing suggestions of the magnificent figure he had seen once and still remembered. Her Nordic beauty had suffered in this past week, however. There were ugly bruises on her face, and for all he knew, equally ugly scars and bruises on her rich body.

Her blue eyes flashed with shocked recognition, and then she bowed her head and tried to hurry on.

"No hard feelings," said Durell. "You remember me, don't you?"

She looked agonized, wet her lips, and again tried to move around him. El-Raschid said gently: "Alida, whom you call Zuzu, has been punished for certain infractions of our rules. She is not permitted to speak to anyone. You may go about your duties, my dear."

The girl looked grateful, shot Durell another look, and hurried on. Durell was pushed ahead by one of the hounds into a huge, softly lighted chamber where the eye was instantly drawn to a thronelike chair with huge oval plaques above it, inscribed in Arabic with writings from the Koran. To the honest Bedouins of Ben-Haakim's tribe, he was sure this place would indeed be considered subverted into a pit

131

of Shaitan. Music floated from behind carved ivory fretwork, the thin reedy wail of flutes and the thud of tambours. The air was softly scented. Servants hurried forward, bowing abjectly, as El-Raschid in his magnificent tunic made his appearance.

"Be at ease," he murmured. And to Durell, he said: "Are you weary? Would you rest and be refreshed, or does your hot American impatience drive you to further examination of my citadel?"

"I came to see all I can," Durell returned.

"But you have had a long journey, a truly trying time. Your friends out in the desert—yes, we know of them—cannot help you, you know. They are no danger to us here, and so we shall let them be, unless they become provocative. On the other hand, I must apologize for the unintentional trials you suffered as a prisoner. It was not meant to be. But even in Paradise, those who dance for Allah sometimes make a misstep. Those responsible were punished, of course. Perfection is not for mortals. They are taught to hope for such achievement in another life."

"And they die willingly?"

"Of course." El-Raschid's smile was thin and cruel with irony. "Just as my little community of scientists works willingly to create the world I shall command."

"Out of fear? Or due to your drugs?"

"Some of both, I admit. And a little surgery often helps. Come, you will see for yourself."

For the next hour, Durell was taken up and down the honeycomb of corridors and chambers, some elegant, some antiseptically simple. Everywhere there was an ominous sense of hurried activity. In one room he recognized Dr. Paolo Nardinocchi of Italy, and Kingsley-Smythe, the rocket fuel expert of London; in another he glimpsed Professor Anton Novotnik of Czechoslovakia, and Dr. Sung Laio, of Communist China. They were all busy, with single-minded purpose, in their various laboratories.

"You seem to be pushing for something," Durell said to El-Raschid.

The big man smiled. "We are ready."

"For the end?"

"The end of the world as you Westerners know it. Come, you shall see the ultimate weapon now, in miniature. Dr. Steigmann proved to be the expert trigger we needed."

"Did he cooperate with you?"

"Now that his daughter is in our hands, he had little choice. He is a sentimental man, but brilliant in laser techniques and weaponry development. We had Francois LeBec here, the French optical man, and Dr. Okira Mayashi. But LeBec, the silly fellow, became recalcitrant. The lobotomy we performed was not a perfect work of surgery. He had to be killed."

"You induce these great scientists to work for you by surgical means?"

"We make them amenable to suggestion, you may say. It was really Bellau's idea. He knew each man's failing—and they are human, after all. It was either money, food, women —we pander to all their tastes—or surgery as a last result. Bellau's files were invaluable in this respect."

"Bellau." Durell paused. "He was your partner from the beginning, then?"

"In many ways. I found it amusing that you and your Western intelligence agencies depended so heavily on him and his dossiers."

Durell nodded. It was clear now. Somewhere in this palace of a Thousand and One Nights was his real enemy, the evil genius who no one had recognized in Munich. Bellau! He felt rage rise and then subside in him. He could allow no emotion to sway him now. Time was running out. It amused El-Raschid to reveal everything to him, but there was no mistaking the quality of anticipation and preparation that filled the air here. Something was going to break—soon.

He considered his chances. The hounds were alert, as always—monomaniacal in their watchfulness. El-Raschid's geniality was sinister in its cheer. Obviously, he was not going to be permitted to see Lisl. He might have to sacrifice her, if forced to make his play too quickly. Simon wouldn't like that, and when he thought of the major and his vengeful Bedouins, he hoped they would somehow find the rumored entrance to the natural caves that tunneled this mountain, and at least create a suitable diversion. But he could not count on that. He was on his own. He had walked like a fly into the spider's web, and the path ahead looked sticky indeed.

They passed more girls, some in servants' clothing, plain blue and shapeless, with dull eyes and sullen mouths. Others wore the filmy accouterments by which El-Raschid had recreated the fabled era of Islam's Caliphate glory. They all looked like drugged automatons. The only one who had shown a flash of intelligence and independence was Zuzu,

133

whose real name apparently was Alida. He filed the thought away for future reference.

Torture and "persuasion" had created a small empire here, headed by a madman and his dwarf accomplice. The eagle and the toad, in league with each other, to gobble up an unsuspecting world! Durell's stomach churned uneasily. No one in Washington suspected the true enormity of the movement that had gathered its momentum in this place. No one was alerted.

He was alone in a world of insane dreams and deadly design.

Chapter Twenty-four

HE SLEPT uneasily. The bed was a soft divan covered with silk and brocades, in a chamber that might have been in a sultan's palace. His mind struggled to recall all that El-Raschid, in his pride, had shown to him. There was a surgery, gleaming and antiseptic, where a tiny, faintly humming laser was being manipulated by a white-smocked surgeon, to act in place of a scalpel in a brain operation on yet another unfortunate, captive mind. And from an opening in the craggy walls of Djebel Kif, he had seen a much larger version of the laser beam gun, surrounded by a crew of technicians who were rapt in purposeful activity.

"Does it really work?" Durell had asked El-Raschid.

"It will shine invisibly, like the sword of Allah, and cut a path through the cities both east and west of this place, as a demonstration of our power. It will not take much, if your Western conscience troubles you. A few million people, who will die by incineration so swiftly they will never know it, is a small sacrifice to show the world what I mean to do. You wince at the number? But people are cheap. There are so many of them now, on this small globe. It is the illness of your times, this lowering of moral standards everywhere in the West, because, with such a surplus, the value of human life goes down."

"One small atomic bomb will make Djebel Kif only a memory," Durell had suggested. "How long do you think it will be before a SAC bomber or a rocket comes over to put an end to it?"

"You truly think so? But what of the diplomatic furor, the U.N. debates, the embassy messages, back and forth, until the time for action passes and the movement has gone beyond hope of any recall?"

Durell had been silent. He knew the truth of the man's words. In today's state of the world, swift reprisal was almost beyond hope. Too many factors—world opinion, blind retaliation, the endless arguments and charges and counter-charges, the enigma of what was really happening—would stall any such hope as he had suggested. El-Raschid was right. The enemy would win, if he got in the first blow.

But he could not let it happen. Somehow, he had to stop it.

As he sat up, there was a light rap on his door. He called out in English to come in, and Zuzu—or Alida—entered, carrying a breakfast tray, with an ornate brass coffee pot, croissants, fresh butter, English jam, fresh scrambled eggs. He was enormously hungry. He started out of bed, realized he was nude, and used the silken sheet to cover himself. The girl paid no attention. He looked for his shoes at once, thinking of the tube of nerve gas in his left heel. They were gone. Soft Moroccan slippers waited for him, and he groaned inwardly, but showed nothing on his face.

"Good morning, Zuzu. Or is it Alida here?"

"Alida is my real name," she replied tonelessly. "Alida Johannsen. But I am not permitted to talk with you. I was sent merely to bring your breakfast."

"Does everyone get this royal treatment?"

"Not at all. You are highly privileged."

"You're the only one around here who seems to be allowed full possession of your faculties. Why is that?"

"It amuses the Prophet. I must go now."

"Wait a moment, please."

"I cannot. I'm afraid."

"What have they done to you?"

She shuddered. The bruises he'd seen on her face were fading, but there was a dead look in her lovely eyes and a lack of hope there that he did not like. He gave her his most disarming smile.

"You don't really think the Prophet is touched by the divine, do you, Alida?"

135

"He is a man," she said bitterly. "He taught me that—as part of my punishment."

"But what did you do to displease him?"

She shrugged. She wore her hair loose, except for a blue-beaded band that held the long, golden strands in a heavy braid down her back. He had not really had a good look at her during those hurried moments in Munich, over a week ago. She was a remarkably beautiful girl. Her Scandinavian eyes were of the purest blue, and her figure could have been that of a Norse goddess of the wild seas.

"How did you ever get into this mess?" he asked.

She shrugged again. "Like most of the other girls here, I wanted to dance, to be in the entertainment world. I answered an advertisement in Stockholm and was recruited for a traveling entertainment troupe, and little by little became a part of the Dancers."

"Didn't you ever try to get away?"

"Just once. After I—I obeyed orders and drugged you, in Munich. It was not the first time, but something about you— I don't know—I determined it would be the last. Then I heard about that poor English girl—Miss Bainbury?—and the disappearance of Lisl Steigmann. Up until then, I did not allow myself to think of the significance of what I had to do for the Dancers. But it was too much. Too much. I am not a saint, or an angel—life has been very hard, and I was very ambitious to succeed, at whatever cost. But after all that, in Munich—well, I had a change in heart. Can you believe it? I thought until then I would do anything to succeed. I thought I was—how do you say it?—tough. When I read Inspector Bellau's name in the newspapers the next day— after I drugged you—I went to him, meaning to tell him everything. But I did not know he was part of the organization. I was stupid, an innocent fool—and I thought I knew the ropes, as you put it. Bellau brought me back. I had no chance. And there will never be another chance. I will never try to get away again."

"Do they frighten you so much?"

"All the girls are terrorized. Then they grow used to the life. Most of their 'work' is to keep the Dancer guards and the scientists content and happy, do you understand?"

"And you? You're meant for El-Raschid, personally?"

She would not look at him. "Yes," she whispered. "I must go now."

"Just another moment—"

136

"They hear and know everything. I cannot help you, if that is what you are going to ask."

"Is every room bugged?"

"And monitored by television."

Durell pursed his lips. "Very efficient. You wouldn't happen to know what's on the agenda for me today, would you?"

"You will be persuaded—brainwashed—like all the others. You will—change. You will serve and obey. El-Raschid expects to gain much information from you."

"Today?"

"Or tomorrow. They are very busy today."

He thought of Simon and his Bedouins. "Was there no alarm or excitement last night, while I slept?"

"Nothing."

Scratch another hope, Durell thought. He let her go, but he did not mean to forget her. All at once, he felt ravenous again, and ate the breakfast she had brought with a hungry appetite, hoping there were no preliminary drugs in the food or coffee.

The twin Dancer guards appeared twenty minutes later to escort him to Dr. Hubertus Steigmann. Durell did not question El-Raschid's motive in giving him this freedom. The eagle and his toad associate, Bellau, had their own reasons and methods of digesting what they snatched up. He hadn't seen the treacherous Bellau as yet, but there would come a moment of reckoning, somehow, he swore to himself. . . .

He was crowded into the golden birdcage of an elevator and whisked swiftly up to the top levels of Djebel Kif. Not for an instant did the twins relax their vigilance. Without words, they urged him down an antiseptic corridor and through a doorway into Steigmann's assigned workshop.

It looked innocent enough. His first glance revealed what seemed like a simple black box attached to a long dark tube that could be pointed like an old-fashioned cannon out of several open ports in the mountainside. But enormously heavy cables were attached to the mechanism, and he supposed the power source was the atomic plant buried deep in the bowels of the eyrie.

Steigmann was too engrossed in his work to notice his arrival. The bearded laser expert seemed harassed, as if too much pressure had been exerted on him to hurry the job. Durell wondered briefly what he had been told about Lisl.

He didn't doubt that Lisl's capture was the main factor in Steigmann's submission here.

"Doctor," he said mildly, "we seem to have been granted the boon of an interview."

Steigmann looked up, startled, and peered at him through thick magnifying lenses; then he took them off with an impatient jerk of a shaky hand. "You here? I thought they had killed you, Herr Durell."

"I'm the stubborn, persistent type, I guess. I kept on following you."

"That was foolish. Go away. Can you not see I am busy?"

"I think we're meant to talk," said Durell. "And our listeners would be annoyed if we didn't."

"Listeners?" Steigmann seemed puzzled, then he glanced at the walls. His assistants, a Japanese and a small man who looked Italian, stepped back like robots too thoroughly programmed for obedience to interfere. Steigmann waved impatiently. "Yes, yes, no doubt. But I have my orders, you know. I must complete the prism balance before nightfall."

Durell asked innocently: "Something gone wrong?"

"The blundering idiots who worked here knew nothing, nothing! And now there is so little time!"

"When is it to be triggered?"

"By nightfall, I told you!" Steigmann seemed shrill in his desperate impatience. "What is it you want to know?"

"Can you tell me what is to be the first target?"

"Ach! Look out there."

He gestured to the portholes cut through the solid stone of the mountain cave. Durell walked carefully by the long laser tube to peer out at the outer world. He patted the tube negligently. How many volts would it take? A million? Ten million? He did not know the size of the atomic generator. But it would be enough. Power had been the prime obstacle in development of this futuristic death ray. Twenty years ago, it would have been scoffed at as a fictional dream. But today spaceships and missiles were only too real, along with supersonic jets and spying satellites. Nothing was impossible. The imagination of man had gone beyond all horror.

From the port, the cliff dropped sheer for hundreds of feet to the foot of the mountain. No way out here, he thought grimly. Beyond, his eyes were all but blinded by the glare of the desert sunlight on the tumbled wastes of the Sinai. Nothing moved out there. All the way to the horizon, there was only empty desolation. He judged from the morning sun

138

that the laser gun was directed to the northeast. Toward Israel, then. Which city was the target? Tel Aviv? Jerusalem, the shrine of all Western religions? Haifa, the port city? Whichever it was, the Israelis, given any time at all, would retaliate instantly. Their target would be Cairo, their self-announced enemy. And once war was triggered, all the Middle East would be inflamed, a seething cauldron in which the Second Prophet could fish for support and alliance.

At this height, he thought he might glimpse a hint of Simon and his Bedouin camp. But Simon was too good a desert campaigner to permit his position to be spotted.

Of course, El-Raschid knew they were in the neighborhood, and would do something about it. Or, in his arrogance, did he think it was unnecessary?

Hard to tell.

He turned, musing, back to Steigmann.

"So you have given up, Doctor?"

Steigmann lifted his head from his work. His round eyes were haunted. "No criticism, my friend. We both should have died some time ago. It would have been better. Then we would not have been forced to make any choices."

"And you've chosen El-Raschid—and this?"

"I could not help myself."

"Is it for Lisl that you commit yourself to evil?"

"I must. My foolishness began this, and it will be the end of it."

"Have you seen Lisl yet?"

The man nodded. "I was permitted this, yes."

"And she's well?"

"Well enough, for the time."

"And if you don't perform on schedule, she'll suffer for it. Is that the ultimatum you got?"

"You know all this. Why do you torture me with it?"

Durell said: "I was just thinking of all the ugly charges against you in Munich. Maybe you were framed, maybe you weren't, for all I know. The crimes that blacken your name are inhuman, beyond the comprehension of any decent, civilized human being. But the crime you're about to commit goes beyond all of them, whether the charges are true or not. This is far worse, past words or description."

Steigmann drew an unsteady breath. His face was an etching in torture. "Do not offer me comparisons or any philosophy. I was innocent, but no one believed me—"

"Your daughter believes in your innocence now."

"No."

"But she does. And what will she feel if she is convinced by your acts here that all the charges against you in the past were true?"

Steigmann put down a chrome-steel tool he was using. His hand trembled. "Am I to let her die, then?"

"Are your lives worth those of millions?"

"I cannot think of that! Is it selfish to want to live? Perhaps so. I am not noble or self-sacrificing. I do not wish to speak of such things. Do not talk to me any more, or I shall call the guards." His face was pale with sweat. "Go away. I must finish my work."

Durell said softly: *"Were* you innocent of the Munich charges?"

"Yes, but what does it matter? I am not an innocent man, in any case. My hands are as bloody as those of Cain. I killed my brother. With these hands, I killed my flesh and blood."

"Your brother was the SS commandant of the camp?"

"Yes. He—he was a monster. I murdered him when the Soviet tanks were within five miles of Offhauzen, and took his papers and fled. I assumed his identity long enough to get back to the German lines. His papers got me through. And when I reached the Allies and requested asylum in the West, I took back my own identity. This is what caused confusion in Herr Bellau's notorious files. So am I innocent? I, who killed my own brother?"

"He was a murderer many times over."

"But I had no right to execute justice for myself! We were boys together, we shared personal memories—"

"He was a monster, as you say, and you did right to kill him."

Steigmann turned angrily. "And Bellau is a monster, too! Why do you not kill him? But he is your ally, you work your espionage nets with him, and you wink at *his* evil! Bah! I am finished with you. Let me work out my own salvation, and let me save my daughter's life."

"You won't save her," Durell said grimly. "We'll all die."

But Steigmann was adamant. He turned his back to Durell and summoned his two assistants back to work. Durell had no idea of the laser technicalities involved. It occurred to him that if he could smash this instrument, the world would gain time in which to breathe again. He considered his chances. It meant certain death for himself, of course—

140

death for all of them trapped in this mountain. The Dancer hounds, with their glittery eyes, might never let him reach the laser tube if he moved suspiciously. A single leap would bring them on his back, scimitars flashing, from their position near the wall. . . .

The wall.

It was different from the smooth tile of the rooms and corridors he had seen elsewhere. The wall they leaned against was of rough-hewn, ancient stones, set in huge blocks without mortar. It was a piece of the crumbling ruins of the monastery atop Djebel Kif. It made sense. In this laboratory, they were near the topmost level of the Prophet's hideout. This wall must be a foundation buttress for the Byzantine structure directly above.

But there was more.

Set in the wall was a heavy door with huge strap hinges of hand-wrought iron, and a massive lock in the center of the planking. The door looked as if it had not been opened for centuries. Probably the key was long lost. Even if it still existed, it was certainly not here in this room. And it was probably beyond the strength of any man to break it open, even if he could get beyond the twins who stood directly before it.

No, it was impossible.

Given the slightest provocation, the hounds would gladly kill him instantly. He had no weapons. And time was running out. How many hours did he have before Steigmann was satisfied with the operation of the laser gun? One? Five? Ten? He'd been ordered to complete his work by nightfall. That left eight hours. But he might never be given a chance to approach this room again.

It had to be now.

Somehow.

At whatever cost.

Chapter Twenty-five

A MUTED bell sounded in the room, even as Durell tensed for action of any kind. He checked himself. The Dancers reacted like Pavlov's dogs to the chimes, murmuring to each

141

other. The Japanese and Italian technicians turned pale and made themselves busier than before. Only Steigmann seemed not to have been indoctrinated to the signal. He kept working, absorbed in his problems.

Then Selim El-Raschid came in. Behind him, toddling on tiny feet, more like a toad than ever beside the giant hawk's figure of the Second Prophet, was Inspector Bellau.

At first, there was something ludicrous about the Munich agent, who looked like a gnomish court jester from some tale of the Caliphate—until you looked closely at the yellow eyes, the warped intelligence that now shone without inhibition through his former mask of suavity. Of the two, the eagle and the toad, it was hard to tell which was more dangerous or amoral.

"Herr Durell," Bellau said quietly. "Have you satisfied your curiosity? Learned enough? We have been most lenient with you."

"It is appreciated," said Durell. "Only the stupid man continues to—" He was about to say "butt his head against a stone wall." He checked himself and finished: "—to struggle against overwhelming odds."

"But wisdom comes too late for you," El-Raschid said thinly. "We have decided about your value to us. Herr Bellau was most helpful in assessing the information you might give us."

"And?" Durell asked.

But he knew the answer. It was marked on their faces, in their eyes.

El-Raschid waved a strong, brown hand to the two Dancer guards.

"Kill him," he said quietly.

Perhaps it was only a subtle form of torture, a trap to judge his reaction. But he couldn't afford the gamble of meekly extending his throat to the knives the hounds flashed at him. He had only one chance.

The laser tube was between him and the Dancers. As they jumped, their knives making glittery arabesques in the air, he slammed his hip against the "muzzle" of the light gun and sent it spinning on its mount to smash into the first twin. As he heard the Dancer on his left grunt with surprise, he put a hand on what would be the breech of a normal gun and vaulted over it, feet first, knees locked. His heels smashed into the second man's stomach. Unfortunately, he wore only the soft leather slippers he had found beside his bed when he had wakened. But the effect was still enough.

The Dancer staggered under the blow and crashed into his twin brother. At that moment, the first Dancer had recovered from the impact of the laser tube and was slashing with his scimitar at Durell's flying figure. The second man staggered between them. There was an ugly *thunk!* as razor-sharp steel sliced through flesh, tendon and bone as if through cheese. Blood gouted as the Dancer's head leaped from his shoulders, fell, rolled, and bounced with wild dead eyes toward El-Raschid.

The first guard screamed in anguish at what he had done. His eyes were incredulous circles of white as he followed the rolling, bumping head of his brother.

Durell slammed the dead torso at him. He had no time to think of the horror in the room. The Dancer screamed again, and Durell heard El-Raschid shout something, and then Durell caught the guard's wrist and wrenched him backward, toward the open port cut through the rock of the mountainside. The man slipped in the blood that gushed over the floor from the severed neck of his brother and fell backward, through the opening. For a frantic instant he clawed at the edge of the wall to prevent his fall. An image of Carole Bainbury's butchered body flickered through Durell's mind, and he hit the man with all his strength. The Dancer screamed a third time and fell back.

For what seemed an eternity, they could hear his shrieks as he fell down and down the dizzy height to the rocks far below. Then it ended abruptly.

It had all taken less than ten seconds.

But El-Raschid had moved fast; his finger was poised to press an alarm button in the wall.

"Don't!" Durell snapped.

The bejeweled figure froze. But Bellau lurched forward on his short legs and reached up, straining, for the button. Durell slammed his weight on the laser gun and again swung it so that its beam, if discharged, would shrivel and wither the dwarf instantly.

"I'd like to do it, Bellau," he said quietly.

"It does not operate," Bellau said. His grin was vicious; his yellow eyes blazed. "You will die soon enough."

Durell turned his head slightly. "Steigmann?"

The scientist stammered: "The p-problem has been one of sealing power loss. The destructive range was limited. However, I believe now—"

"It works?"

"Y-yes, Herr Durell, but—"

Durell found the obvious trigger. He pointed the tube at the ancient wooden doorway in the stone wall and squeezed. . . .

Nothing seemed to happen.

There was no sound, no dazzling flash of light, no explosion. . . .

Then, in a formless instant of time, the heavy panels with their huge iron hinges simply vanished.

There was a gust of invisible heat that seared the senses, followed by a humming, and then a small clattering of molten drops of stone. Dust filled the room and set them all to coughing and staggering. El-Raschid's heavily embroidered robe was on fire, and the man shouted and beat at the flames that enveloped his giant figure.

Where the door had been, there was now a seared hole where molten stone still dripped. Darkness gaped beyond, filled with a strange singing sound that faded even as he became aware of it. Durell took his hand from the laser gun. He could see, as if through a long, long tunnel, a glimmer of light beyond the hole now, where the beam had cut through the foundations of the monastery ruins and even sliced through the opposite side of Djebel Kif's rocky shoulders.

"Steigmann?" he said softly.

"What—what have you done?"

"Come with me."

"Are you mad? You could have killed us all! You are a butcher—"

"Come along."

"I will not leave my daughter in this place."

"We'll get her out later. Bellau!"

The dwarf was trying to help El-Raschid beat out the flames in his ornate clothing. Neither seemed to hear him. It was too much to herd them with him, Durell decided. Without a gun as he was, they would be too great a burden for him. A bell clanged somewhere, and he heard the sound of running feet. Obviously, the discharge of the laser gun, however silent, had drained the atomic reactor far below and signaled a warning to El-Raschid's people. He had only moments to spare. He was committed now.

He grabbed Steigmann and shoved the bearded man bodily through the opening in the wall cut by the laser. The residual heat seared his face as he followed Steigmann's

144

dazed, stumbling figure into the darkness. The man fell to his knees. Durell yanked him up and shouted, "Keep going!" and urged him on. Their footsteps made soft, echoing slaps as they pressed ahead. They were in a vast, gloomy underground vault, perhaps a wine cellar once used by the Dancing Monks a thousand years ago. From behind them came shrill shouts of alarm.

Steigmann gasped: "I must go back for Lisl—"

"It's too late for that now. They'll kill us without mercy."

"But it is impossible to get out!"

"You just achieved the impossible with that laser ray. Now save your breath and keep going."

It was dark here, except for the dim light that came from the room they had escaped and a ray of sunshine far ahead and above them. Stout stone columns rose from the slab floor and flowered into ornate Byzantine capitals overhead. He could not see the ceiling. He pushed the bearded man ahead. Dust lifted around their feet—the residue of centuries. From behind came a shout of discovery and the patter of rapid steps. Durell moved at a diagonal to the opening, putting as many of the fat stone pillars between him and their pursuers as possible. Steigmann stumbled and fell again.

"Get up, if you ever want to see Lisl again!"

"It is no use—"

They went on. The cavernous cellar seemed endless. He headed for the opening in the opposite wall, blasted clear by the laser beam. It seemed high overhead as he approached, and he realized he had aimed the tube slightly upward. The tangent of the controlled beam had cut through the mountainside at an upward angle, and before he was halfway across the vault, he saw that the opening was too high to reach from the slab floor. He swore softly. The noise of pursuit raised loud echoes from the vaulted foof. He thought he heard Bellau's shrill German invectives, urging the murderous Dancers on, but he could not be sure. Was El-Raschid alive or dead from his burns? But there was no time to consider that now. He searched for another way out.

Stone steps against a dark, cold wall led upward to an arched gallery. Steigmann moved faster now, but not fast enough. Flashes of light from torches made an eerie pattern in the gloom behind them. The Dancers were scattering like a pack of hunting dogs on the scent. A shot rang out, but it was only a wild stab at the shadows. Then Durell and his unwilling companion reached the top of the stairs and plunged through an arcaded opening into a tunnel-like corridor. It led them to the right, then to the left, past a series of cubby-holes that must have been the sleeping cells of dedicated monks who had lived out their lives in this remote mountain fastness.

He had to slow down now. The darkness was thicker, gloomier, and he could not see the way ahead.

Steigmann breathed badly, with the wheezing, painful gasp that reflected his laboring heart.

"Stop. *Bitte*. I feel faint—"

"This way," Durell said.

He dragged the man around a corner of the stone corridor. Dim light glimmered ahead, but he could not see its source. It looked artificial, and it flickered erratically. Perhaps the Dancers were coming at them from both directions. If so, they were trapped.

His thoughts jumped ahead. If they were to be captured again, he could not let Steigmann be put back to work on the laser equipment. Above all else, that had to be stopped. The man's genius could not be returned to El-Raschid's unholy scheme. Which left only one alternative. If they were caught, he had to kill Steigmann, rather than let the Dancers use him again. There was no other way.

Perhaps Steigmann realized this. He looked at Durell with dawning horror in his round eyes as he recognized their desperate situation.

"Very well," he whispered suddenly. "I will help. We go this way, to the left. I was here yesterday. I recognize this place. We are near the old garden and pool, overhead. There are stone viaducts where water was collected into a cistern. . . ."

"Let's go."

Steigmann showed him a channel like a broad, hollow trough cut into the wall. It vanished through a two-foot hole nearby.

"Can you get up there?"

"Help me," the man whispered.

Steigmann was clumsy with fatigue. They made it none too soon. Durell shoved him up, then made him lie flat and they huddled in the dry water-course above the corridor as footsteps raced by. There came guttural shouts in Arabic as the Dancers passed and met another squad coming from the opposite direction. Yelps of anger and frustration sounded, then a crisp order. The footsteps scattered in other directions, and Durell raised his head cautiously. The hall was empty. But it was a death trap. He had to find another way out.

"Crawl up through the hole," he whispered.

"I do not know where it goes."

"Into the cistern, probably. Go on."

His guess was correct. There was a long drop, perhaps of ten feet, when they emerged from the hole above a vast pool of black water. The moist air struck him like a slap in the face with a wet towel, but it revived him and helped Steigmann.

"How wide is it across?"

"I do not know."

"Can you swim?"

"I—I will try."

Durell lowered him by his arms and then let go. Steigmann fell with a soft splash into the black cistern. He followed a moment later. He tried to swim silently—the water depth was too great to touch bottom—but Steigmann paddled awkwardly, and the stone ceiling sent wet echoes back and forth through the black chamber. Durell had no idea where to go. But there had to be an intake as well as an outlet, and he swam ahead, trusting to luck. The darkness was not absolute. There seemed to be a yellowish mist ahead, but it was impossible to judge the distance. Then the mist brightened, when he had almost given up, and he caught a glimmer of what seemed to be sunlight slightly to the left and some hundred feet off. The light grew brighter as he urged Steigmann through the cold water. The doctor's teeth chattered.

"Hold on," Durell insisted. "Just a little farther."

"I c-cannot!"

"You must."

The light was tricky. It did not seem to come from the air, but from the water itself, a phosphorescence that now made a greenish glow from beneath the surface. He paused, treading water, and supported Steigmann's increasingly clumsy form. The radiance came from beneath his kicking feet. It was daylight, but it came from below! He could not understand it at first. Then he saw the mossy stone wall rise before him, some ten feet overhead to the dripping, vaulted ceiling of the great cistern. And he suddenly knew its source.

"Can you dive?" he asked Steigmann.

"I am not certain—"

"There's a hole in the wall down there. I don't know where

it goes, but we must swim through it. There is no other way out."

He had almost spent himself, but the thing had to be done. There were crevices in the nearby wall, and he put Steigmann's uncertain hands on them for a grip while he dived down to explore the source of light. He did not make it the first time. He came up, gasping, and saw that Steigmann was secure, and tried again. The rough stones scraped his back painfully. He took a few strokes, saw a much stronger luminosity directly overhead, the reflection of hot sunlight on the surface of the water, and came back again directly. It took three tries to get Steigmann through the hole in the cistern wall.

Then, with several powerful kicks that took the last of his strength, he shot up toward the daylight, towing the bearded man behind him.

For an instant, as his head came into the air, he was blinded by the brilliant sunlight. He could see nothing. He caught Steigmann and kept his head above water. The air was hot as he dragged in a great lungful with blessed relief.

Then, as his vision cleared, he saw a coping nearby and suddenly recalled the pond he had glimpsed when he first arrived atop Djebel Kif. It was near the camouflaged helicopter and the well he had noted standing in a desolate little garden among the ruins of the monastery walls.

He knew where he was, at last.

But as his vision cleared in the bright sunshine, he saw a shape lean over the coping of the pond, dark against the hot sky, and an arm was uplifted to bring a blow down upon his head.

It was the girl, Alida—formerly known as Mademoiselle Zuzu.

Chapter Twenty-six

SHE dropped the bucket she had been swinging at him and it fell with a splash into the water. Her lovely face reflected surprise and bewilderment and fear, all at once. She gave a small cry, quickly stifled it, and shrank back as he extended a hand toward her from the water.

"Help Dr. Steigmann up."

"But—but where—?"

"Never mind. Just help us."

She reacted without thought, aiding Steigmann up out of the pool and over the coping, where he fell prone, gasping, his lips blue; his eyes stared with total exhaustion. Durell followed an instant later.

"What are you going to do with him?" the girl asked. She was bluntly hostile. "Are you going to kill him?"

She was sharper than he had thought. "Keep your voice down," he gasped.

"Are you?" she insisted.

"Not unless we're caught. And that's up to you."

"I can't help. They're hunting for you all over the place." She was pale with fear. "Quick, come in here."

There were some scrubby oleanders and date palms growing in niches along the monastery walls, part of the camouflage that hid the small helicopter nearby. They scrambled into the shelter of the bushes, dragging Steigmann with them. Durell was not sure if the doctor had heard his quick exchange with Alida. But it couldn't be helped if he had. Alida had to be told the truth. If his judgment of her was correct, she might be persuaded to stay on his side.

She still wore the plain blue gown of servitude that denoted her punishment status in El-Raschid's strange world. Oddly, her figure seemed all the more provocative under the simple shift. But her eyes were as haunted as a wild animal's, darting here and there through the greenery in expectation of pursuit.

"Don't you want to get out of here?" Durell whispered.

"It cannot be done," she said at once.

"But you've been here for some time. Is the gateway the only way out?"

"It is always guarded with machine-gun crews."

"That's not my question. Is there another way?"

She shook her head, setting her long blonde hair to swinging, then bit her rich underlip. "I don't know how you got up here through the pond. Every way is guarded, and no one can escape from below. They're pretty sure of that up here, so they only watch for intruders from outside, not for anyone trying to get out. Do you understand?"

"Go on."

She pointed across the pond. "In the ruins over there, the

149

wall is broken down, but the mountainside is too steep to climb down, I'm afraid."

"We'll have to try it," he decided.

She looked at Steigmann with doubt. "Taking him?"

"Yes, he comes with us."

"But he could not make it."

"Could you?"

"I think so, but I used to do mountain-climbing—"

"Then there's only one alternative to taking Steigmann along," he said flatly. "We can't leave him here to finish his work on the laser ray. It's scheduled to be used tonight."

She shuddered. "You can't kill him in cold blood. He's as innocent as the rest of us."

"Then we take him. Come on."

They had to wait while a squad of armed Dancers trotted across the sunlit compound. The helicopter tempted Durell, and he thought he could manage to fly it, having once taken a series of lessons. But it was a futile hope. By the time he removed the netting, the alarm would concentrate every killer in the place at this spot. As it was, they still had a chance, since the hunt was still being made in the labyrinth below.

But the girl hesitated. Her fear of the Dancers was still dominant. "No one's ever escaped from Djebel Kif before. They were all caught, and their punishments were—it was horrible."

"It can't be worse than staying here," Durell urged. "Let's go. It's clear now."

"One moment." Steigmann spoke quietly, and his eyes were clear and calm now. "I wish you to know, Herr Durell, that I concur in your decision. If we are recaptured, you must kill me. Otherwise, they will use Lisl to make me finish their work. But I cannot leave without Lisl. I cannot desert her."

"I'll come back for her as soon as you're safely away," Durell promised.

"That may be impossible. It must be done now."

There was no mistaking the adamant decision that Steigmann had made. Durell knew he could not push the man further. He looked at the girl. "Do you know where to find Lisl?"

"I think so."

"Could you get her up here?"

Alida hesitated. "I don't know. I could try."

150

"How long would it take?"

"Perhaps ten minutes. If there is confusion down there, the guard may be removed from the women's quarters."

"Do you have the freedom to walk about anywhere?"

"Normally, yes. But they may stop me now."

It had to be tried. Time was slipping by. He knew he could push Steigmann no further, and he had to admit being reluctant to leave Lisl in El-Raschid's hands, even at the risk of his assignment. There was always the last and ultimate resort; Steigmann knew the risk to himself, at Durell's hands, if capture seemed unavoidable. But the man's calm determination decided him.

"Go ahead, Alida. We'll meet you when you show up on the other side of the compound with Lisl."

"I can promise nothing. If I do not return, go through that archway over there, and on the other side you will see where the wall is broken. You can get down the mountain-side from there."

Alida got up, carrying her water bucket. Her head was high, despite the obvious fear she felt. When she vanished through a ruined archway beyond the pond without incident, Durell settled down for the longest minutes he had ever known. He glimpsed two Dancers at the main entrance beyond the compound, and knew there were more at their machine guns, staring down the little goat path to the south; but their interest was turned outward, and not to the area behind them, as Alida had suggested.

They waited.

At any moment he expected an eruption of Dancers heading for their hiding place, which would indicate that Alida had either been caught or had betrayed them. The last possibility couldn't be ignored. He waited with mounting dread as time slid by and she did not reappear.

The sky was a clear, hot blue. The sun over their hiding place was enormous, its head like a crushing blow. A single vulture swept in slow circles just to the north of the peak. All else was empty of life. There was no alarm from the labyrinth below. The search had evidently turned downward rather than up here. But their luck couldn't last forever.

Where was the girl?

Why didn't she come back?

He sweated in their close confinement under the oleanders. Nothing had been heard from Simon and Ben-Haakim's tribesmen. Had El-Raschid wiped them out, after all? It could be a form of exquisite torture to break him down and end his resistance. He wondered how badly the Second Prophet had been burned by the heat that enflamed his robes. The man would be in an enormous rage, goaded by an egomaniacal fury for revenge, and there would be no mercy for them if Alida were caught.

Sunlight shimmered on the slabbed courtyard. He watched the entrance where Alida had vanished. No one appeared. Surely more than five minutes had gone by. Perhaps ten. She wasn't coming back. He did not look at Steigmann. Steigmann was gray with tension and fatigue. He knew the risks. Durell began to think of how he would kill the man. He would do it quickly, with mercy. But he had no weapons. It had to be done with his bare hands. . . .

Sweat blurred his vision and he moved with care to dash it from his eyes. When he looked up again, she was there.

At first, he thought she was alone.

Then he saw Lisl following, head bowed slightly, carrying a water bucket as Alida had done. Lisl's face was drawn; she, too, wore a blue smock, and her pale hair was tightly bound at the nape of her neck, giving her a meek and virginal quality.

Steigmann breathed softly. "My daughter . . ."

"Hold it."

The two girls walked across the sunny compound and vanished into a dark archway beyond the pool. The guards at the main entrance did not stir; but then one of them, perhaps hearing their footsteps, turned his head and stared down from his machine-gun post, fifty yards away. He watched them out of sight, then returned to his vigil over the Sinai.

"All clear now," Durell murmured.

The dash across the sunlit area was the worst part of it. There was a panicky desire to stay hidden in the shrubs, to cower there indefinitely and pray they might last out the time until nightfall. But there was small chance they could avoid discovery until then. He had to go on.

They walked quietly, although Steigmann lurched in his haste. Durell held him back with a hand on his arm.

They made it without incident. When they passed through the arch where the girls had gone, the reaction made Steigmann slump to his knees. Lisl came from the shadows with a small, whispered cry and knelt beside her father.

"Can you forgive me? Can you? I've done all this to you . . ."

"It will be all right," Steigmann gasped. "Herr Durell will make it fine, *kleine*. . . ."

Durell wished he had the other's confidence. He looked at Alida, who gestured urgently. She said: "They begin to think down there that you managed to get by the elevator somehow. They will start up any moment . . ."

"Show me this place where we can get out."

Lisl helped her father to his feet. Between them, they hurried down a shadowy corridor, past a crumbly chantry, across a chapel whose roof had long fallen into dust, and then he saw where the stone blocks had fallen away from the buttress wall and the limitless sky and desert loomed beyond.

His hope almost failed him when he looked down the precipice they had to descend. It fell away from the foundation in a sheer drop to a ledge twenty feet below. From there, a slope of broken shale presented tricky footing for another hundred feet, then another ledge might lead them downward. But the first drop was impossible for Steigmann.

"One moment," Alida said. "I took the time to get this." She lifted her smock above her thighs and rapidly unwound from about her hips a long length of nylon rope. Her grin mocked him. "I've thought of this way out before, and hid the rope long ago. But even if we get to the bottom, there is still the desert for many, many miles ahead of us."

"One thing at a time," Durell said. "That's how we'll make it."

They lowered Steigmann first, then Lisl. Steigmann slipped in the shale at the bottom and slid dangerously for a dozen feet before he scrabbled for a grip and checked himself. Dust boiled up about them. The pebbles Steigmann disturbed made a dry rattling sound that seemed enormously loud in the stillness. Durell held his breath. There was no alarm. Dark umber and purple shadows waited below, since this was the north slope and the sun did not shine directly on this shoulder of Djebel Kif. After Lisl reached her father, he lowered Alida. The blonde girl descended expertly. Durell tied a loop around a fallen block of stone and let himself down after her, and when his footing was secure, he flipped the noose away and caught it as it snaked down to him.

The real nightmare now began. Lisl, having lived all her life in the shadows of the Bavarian Alps, was reasonably agile, but Steigmann's strength rapidly ebbed. Each step of the way had to be prepared for him, at constant risk to them all. On the lower ledge, he slipped again and Alida made a small sound of despair. Lisl eyed them desperately. Durell knew their chances of success this way were incalculably small.

153

At the end of the ledge there was another drop, too deep to use the rope, and they had to climb over a small pinnacle that thrust up from the mountainside. Inevitably, their route took them closer to the main gate where the Dancers stood on guard, but it was not yet in sight. Ahead there was another shale slope, and with the first step, Steigmann gave a small cry and went down with a cry of pain as his ankle collapsed under him.

He slid and rolled for a hundred feet, while Durell and the girls fought their way down to him, maintaining a precarious balance. At the bottom, Steigmann clutched his ankle and looked up at them with a gray face.

"I cannot go on. I am finished."

"You've got to," Durell said.

"My foot—take Lisl with you, and end it for me. I am not afraid—"

Dust covered them from their descent. They had gone less than halfway down, through a series of miracles. But it was the end now, if Steigmann couldn't even walk. They had come out of the shadowed edges of Djebel Kif and were in bright sunlight, a light that seared their skin and burned their eyes with diabolical strength. The horizon shimmered emptily in all directions. He could see the goat path by which he had ascended yesterday, and he turned his head just as a rifle cracked above and a bullet whined through the trembling air nearby.

They were in plain sight of the Dancers guarding the main entrance. The monastery walls soared above them like ancient battlements.

"Come along!" Durell snapped. "We'll help you."

He pulled Steigmann up and bodily supported him while Lisl helped on the other side. Twenty yards below were some small, folded ridges that might offer them cover. But he doubted if they could reach them. Steigmann was heavy and clumsy. Dim, ululating cries broke from the Dancers. A machine gun chattered, raising echoes that made the solitary vulture circling overhead lift abruptly into the blinding sky. Splinters of stone stung them as they slid down to the ridges. Durell glanced back over his shoulders. The Dancers came leaping down the mountainside like howling dervishes, shrieking cries of victory. Leading them, moving faster than his followers, was the giant figure of El-Raschid himself, his burned robes flapping like eagle's wings.

There was no escape.

They reached the first ridge and dropped to the hot, dusty rocks, which offered them safety only from direct fire. But it was impossible to outrun their pursuers.

"Durell," Steigmann whispered. "do what you must."

He cast about desperately. There was a crevice in the mountainside beyond the little ridge, a dark and narrow crack in the volcanic stone. He shoved the two girls and Dr. Steigmann violently inside.

"Stay there."

Then he picked up a jagged piece of stone and held it in his fist. The cries of the Dancers were louder now. But nearer than the rest came the quick, accurate steps of El-Raschid.

One way or another, Durell thought . . .

The stone in his hand was hot enough to sear his palm. He thought he heard the scuffling of feet behind him from the crevice where he had sheltered the others, but he didn't turn to look. Every nerve and muscle of his body was concentrated on El-Raschid's approach.

The man leaped high, a giant shadow against the blazing sky, and a steel blade slashed viciously through the air with a thin, flat sound. But Durell had ducked under it. He glimpsed the Prophet's face and saw the ugly welts of burns and the tattered tunic that gaped to show equally serious burns on the man's huge body. His face was demoniacal in his rage to kill. Durell whirled, his sandaled feet skidding in the loose shale, and again the glittery blade thrummed through the air over his head.

He came in close, the stone in his fist, and swung hard. It was a clash that promised death for both of them. In the instant when he slammed the jagged stone into El-Raschid's forehead with all his strength, he felt a shattering blow beside his neck that turned the world into a spinning carousel of blazing sky and rocky desert, pinwheeling away without orientation. He thought he heard shouting nearby, and knew he had both won and lost. El-Raschid was dead. For just an instant, he saw the man's shattered face, frozen in a grimace of hatred and astonishment, and then hands grabbed him roughly and tried to hold him up. But he could not stand up.

He let himself fall, with a feeling of utter despair, mingled with a last wave of enormous relief. The Prophet was dead.

Then darkness swallowed him.

Chapter Twenty-seven

A FACE so old and evil that he could not believe it was human leaned over him and whispered soft, lulling gutturals of commiseration. It was wrinkled, bearded, leathery and toothless. It swayed before him as if on a ship at sea, and his stomach lurched and there was a roaring in his ears. The light was dim. A brass cup was held to his lips. The liquid spilled into his unwilling mouth and tasted like mint tea. He threw it up, and the wracking spasms dropped him back into the darkness again.

When he awoke again, the ship seemed to have stopped. The darkness was made all the more intense by a nimbus of yellow flame that flickered, died, and flickered again. Someone else was bending over him.

"Sam? Sam?"

He smelled the perfume of a woman. He strained to see. His shoulder shrieked with pain and sweat broke out all over him. Mingled with the perfume was the stink of a camel robe that hadn't been cured properly.

"Sam?"

This couldn't be heaven. On the other hand, it wasn't hell, either. The hand on his forehead was soft and cool and gentle. The voice that called him was persuasive.

"You'll be fine, Sam. We're on our way home."

"Home?"

"Yes."

"I have no home."

"We're over the frontier. This is Alida. Can't you recognize me?"

Her face swam out of the gloom. Her hair was soft and scented. Her mouth pressed down on his, her lips lingering. He felt a stir of life in himself.

"The Dancers?" he whispered.

"Simon will tell you about them. It's all over."

"Is Simon here? I want to talk to him."

"Later, Sam. You're badly hurt."

"Now," he said.

She went away, and he tried to stay awake, but he was

asleep before anyone came back. The next time he opened his eyes, he felt better. His mind was clear. A thousand questions came to his tongue, but he was alone in a striped Bedouin tent, and beyond the open flap, he saw the familiar sandy wadis of the Negev and the archaeological dig around the Nabatean ruins where they had started. Everything seemed normal. He did not know what had happened.

There was food and a pot of tea beside the pallet on which he lay. He tried to reach for it, found one shoulder so tightly bandaged he could not move it, and tried the other hand. The pain was not too bad. He began to feel hopeful.

Simon came in a few minutes later.

His bulk filled the tent opening for a moment as he paused, blocking the harsh sunlight. Then he came forward and a rare smile touched his blunt face.

"Welcome back, Sam."

He searched Simon's eyes. "How did I get here? Tell me what happened."

Simon said: "Have you eaten anything yet?"

"Later. Start talking."

"You can eat while I explain."

"What about El-Raschid and Djebel Kif?"

"Wiped off the map. Drink your tea."

"Wiped—?"

"We'd just found the entrance to the natural caves under the mountain when you and Steigmann and the two girls barreled down on us. You killed El-Raschid with that David's blow with the stone, by the way. As for what he did to you— old Ibrahim says you'll live. The Prophet got you with the flat of his sword. If his wrist had been turned an inch the other way, you'd have been picking up your head."

"And Djebel Kif?"

"We blew it up. When the Dancers found El-Raschid dead, they went around in circles in their confusion. They couldn't believe he was really mortal. They sat around wailing, waiting for a miracle of instant resurrection, I suppose. In the meantime, we got all of you into the cave. We found our way down to the atomic reactor chamber and speeded it up so we had a pretty violent explosion. It didn't quite destroy Djebel Kif, but it will never look the same. It's all over, Sam. Nothing more to worry about. I've been on the radio with my own HQ and took the liberty of notifying your man in Jerusalem to come and get Steigmann. He did. Dr. Steigmann is on an El Al jet right now, flying to Washington. As for you,

I told him you needed about two weeks to convalesce and would report in yourself by then—either to him or to Athens. Right?"

Durell did not question Simon's sources of information. "And the girls?"

"Lisl stayed behind. She's fine."

"And Alida?"

"She wants to nurse you back to health, Sam. She thinks you're something a little larger than life."

Durell sank back with a sigh of relief. "Was it Alida I saw here, earlier?"

"That's right."

"A lovely girl."

Simon grinned. "She thinks you're lovely, too. You should have a pleasant convalescence."

Durell looked up at him. "What are you going to do about Lisl?"

Simon was silent, and seemed embarrassed. His rugged face creased with thought, and then he said quietly: "She will stay here. In Israel, I mean. I've tried to tell her she needn't take on all the burden of guilt for what the Nazis did, but she says it isn't that. She says she simply feels that she belongs here."

"With you, Simon," Durell said quietly.

"I'm not sure."

"It's plain to everybody but you that she's fallen in love with you."

Simon was silent again. Then he said: "I hope so." Durell sat up then, heedless of the wrench of pain that went through his left shoulder. His face was pale. "Simon, you say you blew up Djebel Kif?"

"That's right."

"But what about the other men—the captured scientists—Nardinocchi, and Professor Novotnik, and the dozen others who were kidnapped?"

"We got most of them out. Ten, altogether. It was the best we could do. Some of the girls, too. It was strange. Some of them refused to come, even though we told them the reactor was running wild. They'd been brainwashed until they couldn't believe the Dancer program for world conquest had failed."

"I know." Durell sighed. "I saw some of them." Then he said grimly: "There's just one person left I'd have wanted to get my hands on."

"Inspector Bellau?"

"Right. What about him?"

Simon looked unhappy. "Sorry, Sam, he got away. He used the helicopter. The last we saw, it was heading east toward Suez and Egypt. The little monster got clean away. But he's the only one, if that's any consolation."

"He was the kingpin, really," Durell mused.

It was not too good. He hated having loose ends dangling like this. It meant his work was not finished. What he had come to know about Herr Inspector Franz Bellau had grown in meaning and importance with each development in this job. He wasn't finished with the gnome-like genius of evil. Bellau's career was like that of a cat with nine lives. His files were still intact. His personal apparatus still functioned. And he was an enemy of prime importance.

As he sank back on his pallet in the tent, he knew he would see Bellau again. Somewhere. Somehow. And the next time . . .

He fell asleep.

"Darling," said Alida.

It was two weeks later, and they were in a luxury suite in the Hotel Grand Bretagne in Athens. Through the windows, he could see the last rays of the evening sun shining on the splendor of the Acropolis. In the bedroom, dusk had come. He had spent most of his time in bed, except for traveling here, obeying the doctor's orders.

"Darling, don't look so worried," Alida said.

"I'm not worried."

"You're frowning horribly. You're worried about me."

He looked at her. "Well, a little."

"Am I such an ugly albatross around your neck?"

"Alida—"

"Oh, hush. Look at me."

"You're very beautiful."

And she was.

She grinned. "Sexy, too. Right?"

"Right."

"Have I changed so much?"

"All for the better."

He would not have known her as the garish Mademoiselle Zuzu of Munich. He had managed to get an allowance for several new outfits of clothing for her from Mike Xanakias, the CIA resident in Athens. But except for her brief shopping spree and a visit to the hotel's beauty salon, she had not left his side. She looked smart and cosmopolitan, a blonde Nordic beauty whose passage caused all masculine eyes to turn her way. Her rich hair was piled in a sophisticated coiffure atop her fine head, and her wide blue eyes gleamed darkly as she sat down on the bed beside him.

"Have you sent all your reports to Washington?"

"Yes," he said.

"Then you have nothing to do for a time except to get well?"

"That's about it."

"You must not be concerned about me. I've had all I want of the 'entertainment world.' Frankly," she smiled, "I'm homesick. I come from a little village near Stockholm, you know. It's on the sea, very peaceful, very quiet. No sandy deserts there, just beaches and ocean. I have a boy waiting there for me, too. I've just decided to marry him."

"Lucky fellow."

"He can wait just a week or so longer, can he not? Until then, no one will bother us here."

So the telephone rang.

She looked dismayed. It rang again. She said something in Swedish which probably was unprintable. When it rang a third time, Durell felt compelled to answer it.

It was Mike Xanakias. His deep voice boomed in the receiver. "Sam, how do you feel?"

"Just fine."

"Well, there's an 'Urgent' from Geneva from your man there. He wants you in Switzerland—"

"I can't hear you," Durell said.

"But the connection is clear—"

"I'm having a relapse," he said.

He hung up.

It was almost dark in the room. Alida moved closer to him on the bed. Her breath was perfumed and quick. Her long, rich body rested beside him.

"Sam?" she whispered.

"They can wait," he said.

She laughed. "Good."

"Come here," he said.

"But your shoulder—when I do this—does it hurt?"

"Not at all," he said.

THE END

160